Out of the
VALLEY

by Bill Muir

Out of the Valley

Bill Muir

Methinx Publishing

MeThinx Publishing

Methinx Publishing
methinxentertainment.com

Printed in the United States of America
First paper edition by Methinx Publishing
ISBN: 978-1-7347696-6-1

Art & Design:
Contributing Editor: Kathryn Tedrick
Cover Art: Digital Coast Media, LLC

Chapter One

A beat-up old truck with a wooden rear bumper and a never-ending battle with rust, rumbled down a winding, dusty drive, stopping beside a pond that was less than full. Edwin Bartlett, worn and weathered far beyond his 65 years, tumbled out of the ancient pickup and dusted himself off. Heaving a sigh, he gazed at the twelve-inch duct that hung over one bank of the pond. A single drop of water clung to the lip of the duct, teasing him since he knew the prospect of more water was dim. Even if it rained, it would only be a temporary solution.

Edwin's tired blue eyes cast a gloomy glance at the hilltop estate looming over his ranch. Therein lay the root of all his troubles. It was a blot, a disgusting stain on the landscape as far as he was concerned, and a battle he seemed destined to lose.

***

In the barn later that morning, Edwin discovered a flat on the left rear tire of his tractor.

"Dang thing must have run over something yesterday."

Fetching his tools, he jacked it up and grabbing his tire iron, he struggled to remove a lug nut. The wrench slipped, and he sliced open the palm of his hand.

"Ow. Ow. Ow." He dropped the wrench and tried to shake the pain off, but that only made his injury bleed more, so he pulled out a somewhat clean handkerchief and wrapped it around his hand. As he stood up, the jack tipped, bringing the tractor crashing to the ground, just missing his foot.

Although black thoughts filled his mind, Edwin resisted the impulse to react.

Keeping his temper in check was proving to be more difficult lately, but dang if he didn't try his best. Walking over to the faucet just outside the barn door, he unwrapped his hand and examined the cut.

Gonna need a band-aid, he thought. He reached out and turned on the faucet to wash the blood away, but instead of clear cold water, the hose vomited a blast of murky brown water and then sputtered dry.

Edwin exploded. Enough was enough. Storming into the house, he grabbed a rifle and headed off, cursing, toward the hilltop estate.

***

Delicate, perfect lips sipped the clear, icy water from a fountain located in the high school hallway. Seventeen-year-old Brianna Padgett was a brunette bombshell, wearing the latest in L.A. fashion, just like the gaggle of model worshipping teen girls clustered around her. As she quenched her thirst, she noticed the stud, Brad Wilson, starring. Only a year older, his chiseled features, chestnut brown hair, and striking green eyes made many of the girls' hearts flutter. He'd been the subject of conversation ever since moving to their school, voted number one for the best looking guy in every survey taken randomly in the girl's locker room.

Brianna decided to play it cool. She straightened up, pulled out her cell, and began texting a message.

A girl in her group, looking at her own phone, glanced up.

"Yeah, girl! You think he'll ask you?" Stacy tried her best to keep the envy out of her voice.

"Irrelevant. He will be mine, dance or no dance," Brianna replied. She hoped that her show of confidence would be believed by the others.

"Oh, my God." A movement drew Stacy's attention across the hall to Madeline, a sorry-looking, plain Jane classmate dressed in what their group would consider 'homeless couture.' The whole gaggle started cackling. Madeline looked down at the floor and retreated, hoping to avoid another embarrassing moment courtesy of Brianna's clique.

"Hey, Mad, what are you wearing, Macy's or Nordstrom's?" Stacy called out loudly.

Brianna wanted to join in, but she couldn't. She wasn't mean by nature, even though she had to pretend to be, to fit in with the group. She really didn't want to pick on Madeline.

Stacy noticed, and it ticked her off. She turned to Brianna. "What's with you? Is Mad Madeline your new BFF? I don't blame you, she's a class act." All the girls laughed uproariously as if it was the best joke ever.

She was about to respond with something witty but was interrupted when someone tapped her on the shoulder. It was Brad. Brianna hid her surprise and a pounding heart by suddenly becoming engrossed in her phone.

"Hi, Brad," she said, peeking up at him.

"What's up, Brianna. I'm going by your neighborhood today, you wanna lift home?"

Brianna's heart skipped a beat. "Uh...yeah, Brad, that works for me. See you then."

"Cool."

He moved on down the hallway, leaving a glowing Brianna, her mind filled with thoughts of the ride home with Brad.

Stacy, however, was clearly pissed, and she glared at her. "Oh. My. God!" She mimicked Brad with a deep voice, "I'm gonna like...be in your neighborhood." Again the group of girls gave Stacy the attention she craved and skittered down the hall, giggling.

"That was a good one, Stace," one girl called out, looking over her shoulder at Brianna.

***

On North Roxbury Drive in Beverly Hills, Brad pulled his red 2010 Corvette convertible to a stop in front of one of the many gorgeous mansions that lined the street. Brianna hopped out of the car, still glowing, but trying to play it cool.

"Hey, wait," Brad called as she started to walk away.

She turned around and gave him a seductive look.

"You, uh...you got a date for the dance yet?" He asked.

"Not yet," she replied coyly.

"Well, I don't know how that's possible."

Brianna did not know whether he was honest or facetious. "Aw...that's sweet, Brad." She let it hang to see which would play out.

Finally, he said, "Well, look, I thought it might be fun if I had the right company, and I can't think of anyone I'd rather be with."

Her eyes lit up. "Yeah?"

"Yeah, so...you wanna go with me?"

Seeing the hope in his eyes made her even more coquettish. She gracefully walked around the front of the car and stopped next to his door. Then bending over, she kissed his cheek.

"I would love to."

She started to straighten up, but he grabbed her arm, pulled her close, and kissed her on the lips. Brianna tried to smile through it. This was a dream come true. The best-looking guy in school wanted to go out with her and had just kissed her to boot.

"Great! It's a date then."

She returned to the sidewalk and waved. "Bye."

Brad grinned as he watched her sauntering strut up the walkway toward the house. He didn't notice the gardener snarl at her, as she paused at the front door and dug into her purse for keys. Timing it perfectly, she looked up and waved again.

Brad smiled, hit the accelerator, and zoomed down the street.

She stared after him, thrilled and heartbroken at the same time. If he ever found out…. Stepping away from the house, she scampered across the lawn in a different direction. The gardener shook his head and glared at her.

Punk kid, he thought.

***

Brianna hurried through the private yards, avoiding barking dogs and angry homeowners to leave the area. Hoping no one, she knew at school would see where she was going. She'd been able to keep her secret for some time now, but she lived in constant fear of discovery.

Increasing her pace, she hoofed it, careful to avoid traffic and tripping on the occasionally exposed tree roots and uneven sidewalks. When she reached Olympic

Boulevard, she climbed the dirty, poorly lit stairs to her rickety, second-floor apartment. Reaching the top of the steps, she walked toward the last apartment on the left. But as she did, Madeline stepped out of an apartment just ahead of her. A jolt of fear raced through her as they spotted each other.

This was Brianna's biggest worry, would Madeline tell? If so, it would ruin everything. Stacy would rip her to pieces and make her an even worse laughing stock. Madeline stared her down as Brianna passed silently by and entered her apartment.

***

The place was a dump with minimal furniture, and that was used, discarded by others who'd left it on the curb for trash pick-up. Brianna dropped her bag on a worn, ripped couch and sat down at a card table in the dingy dining area across from a woman already seated there.

"Hi, Mom."

Brianna's mother, thirty-four-year-old Adele Padgett, wearing a cheap gold plated choker, denim Capri's, and dirty white t-shirt, had her arms wrapped around a plastic bottle of Aristocrat Vodka. A ghost of a woman, weighing less than a hundred pounds, she leered at Brianna through heavy eyelids.

"You scab a ride today? I'm damn near about starving here."

Brianna nodded. Rising, she went to the cupboard and pulled out what she needed to start cooking some rice. It was cheap and filling, often the only thing that kept their bellies full. She could have been an angry, rebellious daughter. Her mother was a worthless has-been, more interested in drowning her sorrows in alcohol than in trying to provide a stable home for her child. Her birth had been an accident, something her mother brought up often. She knew she was unwanted, even as an infant.

From the time she was very young, Brianna had to take care of herself. Later her mother as well, when her faltering acting career had finally tanked for good. Brianna, however, was considerate and good-hearted. Despite everything, she loved her mother and did her best to do what she could in a difficult situation.

As she added the rice, water, and salt to one of the two beat-up saucepans they owned.

Returning to her chair, she decided to try to talk to her mom like any other girl might do with her mom.

"There's this guy that just started going to our school. He's so hot. I can't believe it, but he seems to like me. He's taking me to the dance, Mom. Major score."

"For now." She paused and gave Brianna a small smirk, "So, the new boy thinks the mansion's yours, huh?"

Brianna remained silent. She hated being deceptive, but she was determined that her life in high school would be different from middle school. The shame she'd dealt with in the last apartment, the one she'd grown up in. If that meant pretending to be someone she wasn't, then that was what she would do.

Her mother raised the bottle and gave Brianna a grin. "Good. That's my girl!"

Chapter Two

The Medford General Store was an old, dusty, but a well-kept establishment. It sold a little bit of everything from canned and boxed food to personal care products, tools, weapons, ammo, and even some clothing. Forty-Eight-year-old Shirley Watkins was busy stocking new merchandise. She also worked the cash register that day. This was usually her day off, but until they hired another clerk, she was stuck.

When Edwin pulled up and entered the building, he was still brooding over the low water level in his pond and his fresh wound. His visit to the estate above his farm had been a waste of time. It had left him even angrier because the owner refused to be baited. He had just acted aristocratic and superior, barely giving him the time of day.

"Afternoon, Ed," Shirley called out as she looked up.

"Shirley," he replied with a nod as he headed straight for the hardware section and grabbed a couple bolts. On his way back to the register, two rowdy kids spilled into the store, laughing and joking around. One of them pushed Edwin, nearly toppling him over. The bolts popped out of his hand and tumbled to the floor, rolling in different directions.

Fighting to keep his cool, he struggled to retrieve them. " 'Scuse me?"

"Yeah, right," a tall, skinny, pimple-faced boy sneered.

His companion, shorter and overweight with a mop of unruly blond hair, saw Edwin going for a bolt. Just before he could grab it, the kid kicked it a few feet away.

"Excuse me," he mocked in a girly voice. He and his friend laughed and headed for the soda cooler.

"Mind your manners while you're here, or I'll toss you out on your ear," Shirley yelled at the troublemakers.

The boys mumbled under their breath but didn't dare sass back. They knew she was a tough lady who could do exactly what she threatened to do. Besides, there was nowhere else in town where they could buy a cold soda and a snack.

"I'm sorry, Edwin," Shirley apologized. "Kids these days have no respect for their elders."

After retrieving the bolts, Edwin set them on the counter. "Not your fault."

Shirley picked up the bolts, placed them in a small brown paper bag, and set it on the counter in front of him. "You can have 'em, on us, sweetie."

Subduing his indignation, Edwin pushed a five-dollar bill toward her. He was a proud, hardworking man, who worked for what he wanted and did not want charity or pity from anyone. At the look on his face, she rang up the transaction and handed him his change.

"Where's Cassandra?"

Shirley shrugged her shoulders. "Cassie has been gone just over a couple weeks now, honey. Nobody knows where. Just gone."

Jed Smith, 54, a ruggedly handsome farmer with dark brown hair and animated blue eyes, strolled in while she was speaking.

"A damn loss, too, I tell ya," he said, walking up next to Shirley.

"Is that so?" Edwin remarked. "Isn't that a shame."

Jed elbowed Shirley. "Sweetest girl in the valley."

"Now, don't you go on, Jed," she began.

Taking advantage of the distraction and not being too bright, the tall punk held up a box of Depends. "Hey, gram-pa!"

"That's it. Out with you!" Shirley yelled. She grabbed a broom from behind the counter and started after the boys, who skedaddled out the door.

Jed had to stifle a giggle. He hid his mirth as Edwin gave him a firm handshake, a stiff smile, and headed out.

"Afternoon, Jed. Shirley."

"Oh, now, what do they know?" Shirley said apologetically as he headed out the door. "They're just a couple of stupid punks. Don't mind 'em, Ed."

Furious, Edwin marched toward his pickup, pulling a Bowie knife from its sheath on his belt. Without slowing, he passed the kids' Mustang and plunged it into one tire, ripping it open.

Surprised and angry, the tall kid shouted, "Hey!"

***

Back at the ranch, the tractor was right where Edwin had left it. He ignored it and headed for the lawnmower, which he fixed with the bolts he had purchased. Then he moved to a workbench where he poured seeds into an odd-looking, homemade crusher and turned the crank, churning them up and producing an oil that dripped into a container. When it was full, he poured the mixture into the mower's gas tank and yanked the pull cord.

The mover sputtered weakly and died. Repeated attempts brought the same results, and then nothing.

Grumbling under his breath, Edwin shoved the mower away from him, knocking it over violently. Just then, Sheriff Allen Woodbridge pulled up and parked his cruiser outside the barn doors. Edwin knew what this was about.

"Edwin."

"Aw, Al."

"I hate to be the one."

The sheriff shook his head in regret. The two men had known each other for a long time. He hated what was going on, but the matter was out of his hands. And the law was the law.

"You know I would never..." Edwin began.

"Dang it, Edwin, you just can't go around doin' that kinda thing. It ain't the Old West anymore."

"Oh, for Pete's sake, Al, of course, I'm not gonna do...It's an act! Somebody ought to shake that thieving, smug-faced so and so."

Woodbridge turned toward the estate looming above Edwin's. "You wanna tell him that yourself?"

"He's killin' me here. You know that."

"It's called threatening people, and you can't do it, Ed. If you do, I'm obligated to step in and intervene."

"Well, what am I supposed to do? The man's trying to force me off my own land!"

"Unfortunately, unless you can prove he is doing something illegal, my hands are tied. Did you take your gun?"

"Course."

"Well, there you go, Ed. I mean, what did you expect? You know what's right and what ain't." He shook his head and walked back to the cruiser. "Next time it'll be my butt if I don't bring you back in cuffs. Don't tempt me, I'm warnin' ya."

"Allen. I got no water!" Edwin shouted as the car pulled away. Alone now, his shoulders sagged. "What am I supposed to do?"

***

At a Beverly Hills Mall, Brianna and Brad left the food court arm-in-arm, happy and infatuated. Approaching a formal wear shop, she motioned for him to wait outside the store, but he ignored her, so she shoved him out. It didn't work, he insisted on coming inside with her. Pulling out some cash, she said, "Brad, baby, would you be a doll and fetch me a latte?"

"Okay...." He would go, but it was clear that he was a bit miffed. He had been anticipating a fashion show where he could enjoy watching her showing off her figure in all the pretty gowns.

Brianna cast Brad a flirty glance through the glass as she perused the dresses. She quickly settled on one, and when she noticed that Brad was out of sight, she breathed a sigh of relief. *Finally,* she thought.

Moments later, she exited the store and hurried across the mall, where she spotted Brad clear across the food court at the Starbucks. Out of sight from the formal wear shop, she pulled the dress from her colossal purse and grabbed him.

He handed her a latte and stared goggle-eyed her "purchase." She showed him the tag, making his jaw drop.

"You little thief!" He exclaimed.

"What? I did not!" Brianna tried to hide her guilt, but why else would she have

14

the dress in her purse instead of a bag?

***

The sun was just setting when Brad drove down North Roxbury Drive in Beverly Hills and pulled his Corvette up to Brianna's lie. She got out with her bag over her shoulder, tucked firmly under her arm.

Further up the sidewalk, Madeline, who was walking home, spotted Brianna ahead and froze before ducking behind a bush where she could watch the proceedings. She watched as Brianna kissed Brad, gave him a little wave, and slowly started up the walk toward the front door. Brad watched her gently swaying hips.

She waved again, but he did not drive away. Reaching the door, she dug around in her purse for her keys and looked back. Brad smiled at her. She smiled back. He still did not leave. She began to sweat. If he waited until she opened the door, she was sunk. She had no way of doing that since this wasn't really her home.

She tried bravely to keep the tremor building within her from her voice. "Where are those keys?" She said loud enough for him to hear.

Then things got worse. The gardener rounded the corner of the house. Seeing her, he dropped his tools and marched toward Brianna, furious.

"Oh, God, help," she muttered under her breath. If the gardener started shouting at her, her secret would be out. No more friends, no more happy life at school, no more Brad. Then, mercifully, he drove off, and not a moment too soon.

Suddenly, the husband and wife homeowners whipped open the front door. The wife attempted to pepper-sprayed Brianna, who, startled, jumped out of the way just in time and raced away.

"For the last time, little missy, get off my porch!" The wife shouted at the fleeing figure.

"There are laws, you tramp!" The husband yelled.

Madeline sneered but waited until the coast was clear before coming out from behind the bush. It was time for some revenge.

***

When she arrived home, Brianna entered her apartment to find her mother passed out on the floor. She dumped her bag on a chair and pulled her mom over to the couch. As she did, Adele involuntarily, unconsciously vomited, soiling not only the floor but her daughter's leg as well.

"Eeeww!"

She went to the kitchen for some towels. As she cleaned off her leg, she noticed a yellow slip of paper that had fallen off the table and landed on the linoleum underneath. Picking it up, she read what was printed on it: *Eviction Notice.*

"Not again!"

Feeling hopeless and disgusted, Brianna drifted out of the apartment. She sat on a step of the front stoop with her iPhone. This was the third time in the past year they had lost their home, and she wondered for the umpteenth time, *why can't she just stop drinking and become an ordinary person like everyone else.*

Chapter Three

Edwin unwrapped the garden hose from its holder and pulled it out to fill a pail. Turning on the faucet, the water started running, but a moment later, it sputtered violently. Muttering under his breath, he fumed until Sheriff Woodbridge's cruiser rolled up to the house.

***

The kitchen in the old farmhouse was typical of its kind. With Shaker-style cabinets painted blue, medium brown wide plank flooring, white tile backsplash and Formica countertops, and white porcelain appliances. Blue and white checkered curtains hung on the windows. Edwin and the Sheriff sat in ladder-back chairs at the birch table in the eat-in kitchen, finishing their lunch.

"Mighty good, Ed," Allen said as he wiped his mouth with a napkin.

"Mm. Enjoy it while you can." Edwin set down his fork and drank some coffee before continuing. "We'll have to start eatin' at your house 'fore too long."

"That'd be fine by me. My Jenifer can whip up a fine lunch for us."

Edwin scowled. It wasn't all right by him. The two men had known each other since grade school. Once a week, since Allen had first become a deputy, they had enjoyed lunch together at the farm. Continuing the tradition even after Ed's wife had passed away from a heart attack.

"Look, Edwin," Al began but was interrupted.

"What am I without this place? This is me here, every inch of it. A man ain't nuthin' without his land."

"Is that so? Well, you know what your wife would want you to do in a jam like this."

Edwin scowled. "Yeah, an' look where it got her."

Woodbridge stood up, collected his hat, and moved toward the door. "Sendin' around a little petition now an' then couldn't hurt."

"You can waste your time if you want, but not mine. No piece of paper with a bunch of signatures is gonna stop him from gobblin' up this entire valley. You mark my words, Al. Gonna end up like some giant farm conglomerate. You think all the good people here are gonna want to work for it? No siree. Ain't like workin' your own land. Be no satisfaction, no fruits of your labor, just a paycheck that will have to be used to buy your food from someone else."

Woodbridge understood. He knew these people, knew that the land was their life's blood, the reason that carried them through all the hard work that filled each day of their lives. Still, his hands were tied. There was nothing he could do to change the situation. With a nod, he left his friend to his bitterness.

Edwin cast a cold glance upward. Something had to be done…and soon.

***

The following Monday at Valley High School, Brianna strutted through the hallways on Brad's arm. She was on cloud nine until they reached her locker, where she froze. It was wide open, and a mob of girls, her so-called friends, were gathered around it. Cackling at a mass of photos plastered inside the walls and door of her locker - photos of Brianna at her low-rent dump.

She blanched, and so did Brad, but he quickly turned and started laughing with the wolves. Stacy handed him one of the photos - a picture of Brianna helping her drunken mother up the staircase.

Not far from the crowd, Madeline smiled nastily at the mortified girl.

Brianna knew who had done this to her, and when she saw her, she marched up and slapped the girl across the face. "Way to Photoshop, swine!" Breaking into tears, she ran down the hallway and out the door of the school.

***

She continued to run all the way to her apartment. Still, as she drew closer, she found the building surrounded by the flashing lights of several police cars, a paramedic van, and an ambulance.

Inside, Adele lay face down at the bottom of the stairs, motionless in a puddle of vodka, her hand still clutching the bottle.

Fear clutched Brianna's heart as she approached. Somehow, she knew what she would discover. It was something she'd had nightmares of for years. Running through the front door of the building, she was horrified when her fears were realized, but a police officer intercepted her.

"You need to back away, miss. Make room."

"No! That's my mother!"

"I'm sorry, miss. You can't be here!"

Another officer hurried over to the distraught girl and gently pulled her away.

"No, you don't understand. I have to go to her. I have to take care of her." Tears streaked down her cheeks. "She needs me," Brianna wailed.

"I'm sorry, miss. What's your name?"

"Brianna." The word came out brokenly between sobs.

The police officer, a middle-aged woman with a kindly face, shook her head. "I'm sorry, Brianna, but your mother is gone."

"Gone? No, she can't be. She's right there. Please! I have to go to her."

"She broke her neck in the fall. She's dead, honey. I'm so sorry."

The distraught girl collapsed in the officer's arms.

***

Brianna sat on a plain wooden bench in the lobby of Century City Social Services, numb, her mind blank as life went on like normal all around her. Her world had come to an end. She was alone with no one to care about her and nowhere to live. The landlord and the police had gone to the apartment earlier to demand that she and her mother vacate the premises. That was why Adele had left the apartment in her drunken state and fallen to her death.

Fortunately, the female cop that had helped Brianna and a social worker was able to go back to the building and retrieve her clothing and personal items. What they found raised more than one eyebrow, but without proof of who was the perpetrator, they let it go. Besides, the girl had gone through enough and was facing an uncertain future. They decided that the mother had probably stolen stuff, and since she was now dead, there was nothing that could be done anyway. If Brianna was the thief, they figured that sooner or later it would catch up with her.

As Brianna sat in what she felt was a void, the social worker, a businesslike woman in her thirties, approached and sat down next to her.

"Brianna. Brianna? I have good news. We won't have to take you to a foster home. We can move you right in with family."

It took a moment for the words to penetrate the devastated girl's brain. She slowly raised her head and looked dully into the eyes of the smiling woman's face. "What family?"

***

Edwin entered the Medford Water Master's building. He shoved his way into the office of the County Water Master, Fish McLaughlin.

"Edwin?" Fish asked, looking up from his computer screen.

"I gotta know, Fish, how that man's got any say so over my water. I gotta see it with my own eyes!"

"Well…." Fish stood up, although too slowly for Edwin. Walking over to a file cabinet on a nearby wall, he dug out some papers and handed them over. Edwin snatched them away.

"Well, now...!" He exclaimed at the viciousness of Edwin's reaction. He watched as the old man carefully read through the papers. Knowing what he would find, however, he left it at that.

"Miss Agnes? Jed? How in...?" He looked up at Fish. "I could see Agnes…maybe, but...Jed? Jed sold him his rights?"

Shaking his head in disbelief, Edwin heard his cell phone rang, and he dug it out of his pocket. "Yup." His brow wrinkled, and a look of astonishment crossed his face. "My daughter did what?"

***

The land radiated a dusky, golden glow as the sun settled towards the bottom of

21

the western sky. Edwin sat in a wooden rocker on his front porch, waiting and watching as the Sheriff's cruiser wound down the long drive toward the ranch house. He was still reeling over the news he had received earlier that day. His only daughter died from a fall down the steps. They said she was drunk at the time.

He hadn't seen her in so long, not since that day she had left, run away as far as he was concerned. It had broken his heart, his wife's, too. Pregnant and unhappy with country life, she had headed for the big city to become a movie star. His wife had tried to talk her into staying and having the baby there. They would have gladly raised the child if she was still bent on going to Hollywood. But Adele wouldn't listen. Said she wouldn't doom her child to the deadly dullness of life on a farm.

If only she had listened to them. For a time after having the baby, Adele had managed to get a few bit parts in movies and tv shows. It was easier to keep track of her then. Too much partying had led to an alcohol problem that worsened after two miscarriages, the last one resulting in a hysterectomy. It was for the best. She wasn't taking proper care of the little girl she had. Too many times, Brianna was left alone in dressing rooms or with one of the kindly set workers that didn't mind looking after her for a bit.

Edwin tried to contact her in an attempt to plead with her to come home. When she wouldn't respond, he and his wife tried to take Brianna away from her, but Adele disappeared with her daughter. Without the money to hire a private investigator, they never found her, and he would never see her again. Now this - a granddaughter he had never met. What would she be like? He stood up to meet the cruiser.

Anxious eyes stared out at him from behind the glass window of the car. The sheriff parked his vehicle and escorted Brianna to her grandfather, carrying her two bags. For some reason, she had trouble making eye contact.

"Edwin."

The two men nodded.

"Brianna, this is your grandfather. He's a fine man who will take good care of you."

Her grandfather extended a hand. "Edwin Bartlett."

Brianna returned a limp shake, lame and half-hearted. Edwin was visibly disappointed, but he buried it.

"There's some paperwork, of course, but...well, you get your rest tonight, Brianna. You'll need it." Woodridge touched the brim of his hat and returned to his cruiser, stopping just before he opened the door. "Anything we can do, Ed, you let us know."

Edwin nodded, and he and Brianna stood there a moment, saying nothing and watching the Sheriff drive off. Finally, she turned and sized up her new guardian.

"So, you're my grandfather."

"Your mother was my little girl."

Brianna snorted. "Really?"

"Now, what is that for?" He demanded.

"Tell me about her career."

"She was an actress."

"After that. What was she after that?" When he gave her no answer, she continued. "Yeah, that's about what I thought. No clue, right?"

"Adele left us. We begged her to stay. She wanted a life in the big city."

Brianna crossed her arms over her chest. "That's not what I heard."

"We tried to get in touch, but she disappeared. We didn't have a lot of money to…."

"No, I get it. You and Granny were too busy safeguarding your perfect little Norman Rockwell bubble, here, that I mean, what did Mom expect? That after you exiled her from the family farm, you were gonna drop everything to spend more than a couple days looking for her? It's cool, I get it. She wasn't worth it. She was in the way."

"She hated it here!" Edwin shouted. "We didn't exile her. We begged…."

"No, *we* didn't, you did all by yourself!"

"She left!"

"And she hated it here? I can't for the life of me, imagine why, with all the love flowing all over the place! Is that how Granny bit it? You just radiated so much love that…."

Edwin raised his hand to slap her but dropped it. "You watch your mouth, young lady!"

"I'll do whatever the hell I want, old man, and don't you *dare* try to be a parent now! You had your chance, and you blew it!"

"Listen to me, young…."

"No, you listen! I'm turning eighteen in a couple months, and the second I do, I am out of here!" Brianna shouted as she stormed up the steps to the house.

"If you're such a paragon of virtue, why didn't you look *us* up?"

Opening the door, she spun around and fixed him with a look that would have curdled milk. "Mom said you were dead!" She slammed the front door behind her.

Her words rocked Edwin's world, and his body wobbled, forcing him to sink down onto the porch steps. The emotional pain sliced through his heart like a steel blade.

"Dead?"

Chapter Four

Stiff from age and too much hard labor, Edwin stood in his bedroom and peeled off his shirt. It had been a long day, and he was bone-tired, both mentally and physically. Glancing up at the sound of a door opening, he saw Brianna enter the hallway, carrying a Gucci toiletry bag and wearing pajama bottoms and a baby tee. He shook his head. She was showing a bit too much midriff as far as he was concerned.

"I see you found your room."

She sneered at him but said nothing.

"Bathroom's on the...."

He stopped speaking when he realized that she had already entered the bathroom and slammed and locked the door behind her. Curious, Edwin crept toward her bedroom and peeked inside, taking inventory of her stuff. On the phone, the social worker had told him about the situation Brianna had been living in. The rundown apartment, the welfare checks, and so on.

How did Brianna get her hands on all this expensive stuff? He wondered. He didn't want to think the thoughts that entered his mind next. *Was she a thief? Had her mother been a thief?* He didn't want to believe it. Neither theory sat right with him, but the social worker had hinted at just that very thing. There was no other explanation for it.

Leaving her room, he headed for the bathroom door and put his ear to it. Over the sound of running water, he heard Brianna going off with someone on her phone. *I suppose I'll have to start paying the bill for that phone now, too.* Edwin sighed. He began to knock, but stopped and was about to return to his room. However, the ever-persistent problem with his water changed his mind.

"Don't be wasting the water in there," he shouted through the door. "It's in short supply. Run it too long, and you'll end up with nothing to wash off the soap but dirty water."

Hearing her scream of frustration, he sighed and padded back to his bedroom. A moment later, the water was turned off, and he closed his door.

***

Knock! Knock! Knock!

Edwin was at Brianna's closed bedroom door, fully dressed and ready for another day's work. Outside, it was pre-dawn, dark, but not quite as dark as it had been earlier in the night. He knocked again.

"Brianna."

His granddaughter stirred in her dream state. She heard her name being called, but somehow it seemed like a part of the weird dream she was having. Her mother was calling to her, trying to tell her something important, but the voice did not match up.

"Time to get up, Brianna. We got chores to do. Come on."

There it was again, the voice calling her. This time, though, it brought her awake.

"Come on, Brianna. Time's a passing."

Groaning, she rolled over and looked at her digital clock. It showed 4:01 a.m. Her face scrunched in disbelief. "Go away. It's the middle of the night."

"You don't live in the city anymore. It's time to get up. There's lots to be done before sun up."

Hearing her groan again, Edwin headed into the kitchen to wait, putting away the last of the dishes left out to dry the night before. When he's finished, he listened for any sign of activity from the bedroom. Nothing. The microwave clock now read 4:10 a.m.

Can't stand around waiting until her royal highness decides she's had enough beauty sleep, he thought. Edwin headed toward the bedrooms and approached Brianna's door, but he just stood there a moment, unsure how to proceed. After all, this was all new to her. She'd just lost her mother and had been thrown into a world she did not comprehend. Still, he did not have time to coddle to her, and when he thought about how she had treated him so far, he dropped the indecision and knocked harder. *Ought to be grateful she has a grandfather willing to take her in and care for her.*

Inside her room, Brianna had fallen back to sleep. She jerked awake at the startling sound, her eyelids feeling like they were glued shut.

"Brianna! Chores!"

She moaned.

"Come on, on your feet! There's work to do."

Edwin finally heard her feet clomp to the hardwood floor.

"Part of livin' on a farm is early risin'."

As he marched away, he heard a sound like a voice from the grave. "God have mercy."

"You're tellin' me!"

***

Edwin headed down the front steps and followed the pathway to the barn, but she was not behind him.

"Brianna!"

When he reached the barn doors, he opened them and walked inside. Brianna drifted in after him like a zombie with her phone in her hand.

Edwin took in the pitiful sight before heading for an area of the barn where he stored the feed for the animals. As he walked, he said, "Found a ditch yesterday I can clean out and hopefully create an artery to my neighbor's water. She's offered to share, but while I'm doin' that, livestock still gotta get fed. Your timing is...well...maybe miracles do happen." He heaved a large feed bag up onto a wheelbarrow and turned to look at her. "Conductin' some important business at four-thirty in the mornin'?"

Brianna looked down, holding her phone. She pocketed it, embarrassed.

"First thing you gotta do is feed the chickens."

"Whoa, what? I don't think so."

Edwin ignored her protests and showed her where the chicken coop was and how to fill the feeder with the high protein feed, and spread the scratch on the ground. He put some feed in her hand. "C'mere!"

"What? No, eew."

"They ain't diseased, child. Give 'er a try."

Knowing he wouldn't leave her alone until she did what she was told, Brianna tried to feed the chickens, but in her haste, she spilled some outside the coop. He scrambled to catch the feed.

"Sonofa...! Now listen! Feed ain't cheap! An' we're on our last legs here. Can't afford to let none go to waste."

"Sorry!"

Brianna wasn't bad or unfeeling. She had just been through so much the past few days that she was overwhelmed. Everything here at her new home was so alien that she didn't know up from down. Truth be told, even though the situation she had left at school had been unbelievably embarrassing, she would rather deal with what she knew than what she didn't.

"I know," Edwin said, softening a little. "This must be awfully bewildering to you, but I really need the help. I'm not a young man anymore."

He finished the job, trying to include Brianna, and explaining the best way to do things. Then he led the way back into the barn and turned to her. "Now. See if you can remember where this sack came from. I'll let you put it back."

"You put it back," she said stubbornly. Still, seeing the look on his face, she struggled to maneuver the heavy wheelbarrow to the storage area. When she tried to lift the sack, however… "Holy cow!"

Edwin had looked away, but at her exclamation, he glanced at her. "Sonofa---. Get back. Get back!" Realizing what was about to happen, Edwin rushed over to save her and the sack from severe trauma. He hefted it back to its spot on the ground.

She scowled.

"Gonna have to get some meat on them bones. Yer as thin as a rail."

"Excuse me? No, I've got plenty of 'meat' on these bones, thank you."

Edwin gave her a look of exasperation, thinking about all the expensive stuff he had seen in her bedroom. "Ya ain't in the palace no more, princess. Real people work for a livin'."

"Real people sleep at night. What am I even doing out here anyway?" She started to leave.

"Get back here!"

The volume of his voice startled her, making her stay. Fearing she was too much like her mother, he had decided that he would have to be firm with her. Then an idea came to mind when he passed the stall of a beautiful but elderly Palomino horse. "This here horse was your mother's. She loved riding her every day. Told her mother once that she never felt so free as when she was on the back of Daisy."

Brianna paused at the horse's stall. She felt intimidated by such a large animal, and when Daisy swung her head over the stall door for a rub and whinnied, she backed up a step.

"It's okay. She won't bite ya. Just lookin' for a little affection. Go ahead and rub her muzzle."

Brianna hesitatingly lifted her hand and touched the horse on the nose. A nicker and a nod later, she relaxed and reached up to scratch Daisy's ears.

"You'll have to get to know her first. Maybe sometime later, I'll teach ya how to ride. You'll both enjoy that." He moved over to another huge sack of feed. "Time to feed the hogs. Since you got no meat on your bones, use these." He grabbed a couple buckets and went to work filling his bucket with the feed from the bag, then he stepped aside. "Go ahead, get in there, and fill the other one."

She reluctantly left the horse started filling her bucket, spilling some in the process. Choking back his angry thoughts, Edwin grabbed the bucket and the bag and did it himself. She stood back to watch. When he finished, he pointed to the first filled bucket. "Take that over to the pen and feed the hogs."

She hesitated. *Chickens were bad enough, now he wants me to feed the pigs?*

His impatience getting the better of him, he snatched the bucket away and marched to the pen with both.

"Don't have all day," he grumbled.

Brianna watched him feed the hogs and then storm back for refills, grumbling all the way. He did the job efficiently, masterfully, taking great pride in every detail of the mundane task. When he finished, he turned to explain further, but she was gone. *Dagnabbit, I've got to show the girl more patience,* he thought, regretting his gruffness.

***

By the time Edwin was finished with the chores, soft sunlight had begun to filter through the windows, warming the home. Entering the house, he approached Brianna's door and knocked, staring at the floor.

"Brianna?" He called out softly. "Let's try this again. Come on out and get some food."

Her door flew open, and she stormed past him, phone in hand. "Oh my God, I'm starving!"

Thirty minutes later, Brianna was already at the table, when Edwin placed their plates in front of them and sat down. He had made an especially hearty breakfast of eggs, sausage links, and fried potatoes - an attempt at a peace offering between grandfather and granddaughter.

Not wanting to spoil their meal, he ignored her texting and dug into his food.

Strangely, though, Brianna was annoyed by his silence. "Wow. So, this is how you farmers eat, huh? Remarkable, you're not all total porkers."

"We work it off," Edwin said after gulping down some hot coffee.

They continued eating, but Brianna, now engrossed in her texting, no longer minded the silence. Not used to having someone ignore him in favor of electronic socializing, he watched her text for several moments before interrupting.

"I 'magine, you'll miss your friends…."

"Ya, figure?" She replied as her thumbs quickly punched in the remaining words of her current text.

"…and your mother."

Brianna put her fork and phone down and glared at him. "What do I even say to that?"

"Whatever you want," he replied earnestly. When she didn't say anything more, he added, "the truth is always a good place to start."

"No way." She picked up her fork and resumed eating.

Edwin allowed the silence to drag out a while longer. From what the social worker had said, he knew that her life with her mother could not have been easy. How bad it was, however, no one knew but Brianna.

When the tension was so high that it seemed like something would snap, she relented. "She was my mother."

"Not good enough." He put down his fork and stared and stared and stared at her. "What else?"

But she remained solid as a rock, missile-locked on her breakfast and getting colder by the second. She scratched her forehead with her middle finger. Edwin cringed. At her age, her mother would never have tried something like that.

Outside the window, a huge truck rumbled down the drive. Edwin stood up, snatched up his plate, and hers, even though she wasn't finished, and deposited them into the sink.

"Hey!"

"Need to help these guys setup. Then I'm off to town. Feed the horses while I'm gone. Will ya?"

"You sure I can handle it?" She sneered.

"Just throw the hay into the stalls. A baby could do it."

"What about water?"

It was an unintended kick in the gut, and it stopped him dead in his tracks. He swallowed his angry words and continued out the door before he said something he would regret. Still boiling, he stomped toward the men waiting next to a huge well-digger truck.

"Yer late!"

Brianna approached the window and watched her grandfather show the men where to dig. He waved an angry dismissive hand at the foreman, got into his pickup, and tore off. She grinned.

Chapter Five

Since she had nothing else to do, Brianna went to the barn to take care of the horses. Half working and half texting, she handled the hay gingerly at first, afraid to get her hands dirty. She screamed when a bale fell on her, forcing her to pocket the phone and concentrate on what she was doing.

"Maybe I should just open the stall door and toss the stupid thing in." However, as she reached for the latch, Daisy poked her head over the stall door and whinnied. She backed up a step, still not totally comfortable with the massive beast yet. "If I do that and you get out, Edwin will kill me for losing my mother's horse."

Unfamiliar with horses, she had no idea that Daisy would most likely go into the pasture to graze and get some exercise. Then would come back to the barn, since she hadn't been frightened away.

"Okay, so forget opening the door. But if I have to put this over the top of your gate, you're going to have to back up." She reached up and placed a hand on the horse's nose. "Back up. Go on now."

The palomino did not move.

"Go on, girl. Back up," Brianna tried again, shoving a little harder until Buttercup nickered. "Okay. We'll just have to do it the hard way." Bending over, she wrestled the bale upward and over the gate into the stall, forcing the horse to back up.

"Great. Just fantastic. Stupid hay. I'm living with Old MacDonald. I'm gonna turn into a Little House on the Prairie farmgirl."

She stopped and looked up at the ceiling. "And now I'm talking to myself.

35

Unbelievable."

Looking in the stall, she said, "So you're my mom's horse, huh? She ever get a D.W.I. With you? Is that even possible?"

Buttercup just looked at her while she munched a mouthful of hay.

"Well, come on, is it? You would know."

"Horses cain't talk, Miss," a male voice with a southern drawl said from behind her.

Brianna whirled around and searched the barn until she spotted a full-fledged cowboy. Handsomer than any guy she had ever seen, standing two stalls over in a stall with another horse.

He touched the brim of his cowboy hat. "Darryl's the name. Darryl Floyd."

"Huh," she replied, trying to hide her embarrassment. "Shows what you know."

"Beg pardon?"

"Horses can't talk. Whoever heard of such nonsense?"

Darryl clammed up and turned icy

Brianna didn't notice. "You've obviously never been out of Medford." She approached him, attracted, and enjoying the sport.

Eyes narrowing, he crossed his arms, a slight smile on his face.

"Probably led a very sheltered childhood. I'll bet you enjoy your shelter."

He allowed her to come all the way into his personal space, and as she took in his demeanor, she suddenly found herself unnerved.

"You don't like shelter?"

"W...what do you think you're doing here anyway?"

"Well," he looked at the horse. "I reckon I think I'm shoeing this here horse."

"And why are you dressed like that? Halloween is like six months away or something."

Darryl ignored her as he picked up the horse's right front leg and started to attach the horseshoe. Eventually, he looked up at her. "I was gonna ask you the same."

"What?"

"Them duds."

"My...duds?" She looked down at her outfit and laughed. "Us city folk like to call 'em clothes, quite expensive, top of the line clothes in the latest fashion."

When she received no answer, she grew nervous again.

"Not all cowboys are dumb, Miss...."

She stared at him. "Brianna."

Darryl nodded. "So, Brianna, where's your granddaddy?"

***

Edwin's pickup rumbled down a long gravel driveway, stopping when he reached the front of a ranch house. Turning off the ignition, he got out, approached the house, and knocked. Jed, a balding man with grey and white stubble on his face and wearing blue coveralls and a plaid shirt, came to the door, drying his hands on an old rag.

"Need to talk, Jed."

"Do we?" He asked as he stepped out on the porch.

"You know what's happening."

"You sure bout that, Edwin?"

"Come clean with me, old friend. How long we been runnin' together?"

"Well, sometime now."

"An' haven't we've always had an understanding? Always helped each other out?"

Jed knew what he was talking about, but he did not want to talk about it. It would cause an argument, and he just wasn't able to do anything about it. So, he continued to act like he didn't understand what his friend meant. "What's this all about?"

"Stop it, Jed. Stop playin' dumb! You sold your water rights to that devil on the hill!"

But Jed only looked confused.

"Charles Magnus wants my land. My land, Jed! I don't know why, but he's holdin' up the water, fixin' to dry me out!"

Jed looked queasy, but he remained silent. He'd had no idea this would happen to Edwin.

"Jed? What ain't you tellin' me? I just wanna understand." Edwin's frustration rendered him silent for a moment. "Why would you sell your water rights to that snake?" he said at last.

"I hate it for you, buddy, but my business is my business." In his discomfort, he just wanted to end this confrontation and get back to what he was doing.

"Jed."

"I gotta go. Jane's waitin' for me."

Jed turned to go inside, but Edwin, suddenly furious, grabbed him roughly, and threw him up against the wall.

"Damn it, what're you hidin'? I know you like my own brother, so don't you go an' destroy the best friendship either one of us ever had!"

"What in Sam…?" Jane's voice could be heard as she left the kitchen and headed for the front door. When she saw the two men, she was astounded. "Edwin Bartlett!"

Her voice and exclamation made him realize what he had just done, and he was ashamed and startled by his own hostility. He backed off. Jed entered the house, leaving him standing there, arms hanging at his sides with a hopeless look with his face.

"You keep on like this, Ed, I won't have to."

His words rang out like a death knoll in Edwin's mind. It made him realize that he was like a man stranded on a sinking boat in the middle of the lake. All around the high waves and churning water lived people he had known for decades – people he had trusted and thought were his friends, but it seemed that none of them were willing to help save him.

***

That evening, Edwin and his granddaughter sat at the kitchen table. Each had a plate heaped with fried pork chops, mashed potatoes, and corn in front of them. Edwin's head hung low. Brianna picked up her fork but stopped when she noticed, thinking that he was praying. It seemed to go one forever.

"Are you praying?" She asked at last.

"No." He looked up at her. "Been figurin' how much longer we got."

"Yeah, well, I was just wondering why I have to eat dinner at this table with you every night. No offense, but mom never ate with me." What she didn't say was that her mother was too drunk to bother eating most of the time. She began to eat, but when he did not reply, she continued. "So how much longer 'til you get the boot?"

"I reckon, best case scenario…two months."

"Until what? My birthday, right?"

Edwin looked up. "Why should I care, the way you been acting?

"Depends. I'll be eighteen. A free woman."

"Mm." It was like her words just passed over his head. "We're gonna lose the farm."

Brianna felt a bit hurt. His response made her feel like he didn't care. "Um, what?"

"You see that house on the hill behind us?"

"Yeah! Nice, right?"

"The devil himself lives up there."

Brianna laughed.

"He's bought up folks' water rights so he can force me...us...off my property."

Witnessing his gruffness and mood the past couple days, provoked her next question. "Was it something you said?"

"Probably. I ain't one for backin' down in a fight."

"Over what?" She replied in a snarky fashion.

Edwin ignored her attitude. "Hay is our bread an' butter, Brianna. Without water, we can't grow it, can't sell it, can't stay on the land that's been handed down through our family for generations."

Brianna finished her food and took her dish to the sink. "Thank God! Maybe we can move to a real town then."

It was like a slap in the face. Her grandfather remained silent, his head down. Broken. Brianna was surprised by his reaction, she deeply regretted her words.

***

It was another scorching hot day. Edwin and Brianna were soaked with perspiration and parched as they worked in the middle of the hayfield, by the waterline, at its engine. Edwin wiped the sweat from his brow and showed Brianna how the machine worked.

"Like this?" She asked.

"Just like that." He went on to further explain the machinery. "Besides missin' friends, why are you so anxious to get back to city life?"

"Men. Obviously."

"Ah, that's what I thought." He paused before saying, "Boyfriend back home?"

"Yeah, *had* one. The quarterback. He was *The One*. He was the man every girl wanted. He was rich...strong...and he was mine."

"Tale as old as time. Quarterback an' rich ta boot."

"Yeah. There a problem with that?"

"Somethin' wrong with an honest workin' man?"

"You mean besides the fact that I haven't met any?" She straightened up and briefly pressed her hands into the small of her back. She wasn't used to doing a lot of physical labor. It was taking a toll on her underused muscles.

"What about Darryl?"

Brianna laughed. "I'm not sure I'd go so far as to call him a 'man.' Country bumpkin's more like it."

Edwin's temper flared. "You could learn a lot from a hayseed like Darryl. Lot to be said for simplicity."

"Well, simplicity can be a little vanilla to a big city girl like me."

Her response just made him madder. "Let me tell you something, Brianna. It's a big world out there. It's exciting. Stimulating. And it'll eat you alive."

"If I let it."

"God knows I don't mean to preach, but ninety-nine out of a hundred guys want one thing and one thing only. Once they get it, they could care less about you."

"Gosh, really?"

"I'm dead serious, Brianna. Your mama had you when she was seventeen…."

"Whoa there! Wait a moment. I am not my Mom!" The vehemence of her words gave him pause.

"And I know you aren't, but you can't afford to be naive when it comes to men!"

"Naive! Who's naive?" She demanded, placing her hands on her hips.

"I'm sure good-lookin' boys flock around a beautiful young lady like yourself. An' you know they're on their very best behavior 'round you, whatever it takes to grab and hold your attention, but you've *got* to remember. The more attractive the fleece, the more potential it's a wolf's wearin' it!"

"Gee, thanks for the lesson, but I think I have a slightly firmer grasp on the real world than you do, old-timer."

"What?"

"Try getting out of the sticks for a change. Then talk to me."

Edwin blew up. "You're just like your mother!"

Brianna narrowed her eyes. "I am *nothing* like my mother!"

"You have no idea."

42

He was about to say more when his sleeve suddenly jerked his arm. The fabric was caught in the machinery, and his arm was slowly being reeled in toward the gears. He fought to rip off the sleeve, but he was old, and he could not tear the fabric. Desperate, he tried to pull his arm out of the sleeve, but he wasn't having any luck there either.

"Oh my God! Edwin!" Brianna cried when she realized what was happening.

"Get a knife!"

"I don't know where one is!" She replied frantically.

"In the toolbox!"

She scrambled over to the toolbox and rifled through it, throwing tools aside in desperation. "Where? I can't find it!"

Edwin jerked and pulled, his movement became more frantic by the second as the gears continued reeling him in. Struggling against the constant tug of the machine, he managed to pull his arm out of the sleeve, but he was still in his shirt, getting slowly dragged closer and closer.

"Damn it, Brianna, anything!"

"What! I can't…!" Her movement grew more frantic, and she tore through the toolbox, trying to find a knife.

"Anything sharp!"

"Oh my God! Take your shirt off!"

Edwin fumbled with one hand as he tried to unbutton the shirt, but his fingers were huge from a lifetime of hard labor. "Son of a...!" he shouted as his body was drawn closer and closer.

Brianna was on the verge of tears. For the first time, fear for her Grandfather's well-being filled her. "No, no, no. Not you, too. I can't…can't lose you, too!"

Edwin fought like a bear, while the entire waterline jerked violently. It was a losing battle, and his shoulder was only inches away from mutilation.

"The hammer! Anything!" His voice shook with panic, and fear gripped him hard.

"What? Tell me what I need." Tears ran down her cheeks and filled her voice.

"Anything!! Grab anything!"

"Oh my God!"

She leaped up with a handful of tools, most of them spilling as she raced over to him. He grabbed the hammer and slammed it against the gears, again and again, hammering frantically, wounding the beast, but it kept churning, kept reeling.

Terrified of losing the only family she had left in her life, Brianna felt a strange calm embrace her. She realized that the hammer was too big to jam into the gears. She looked down at her hand and saw a file she didn't know she was holding. Raising it like a knife, she stabbed it into the gears, bringing the monster to an abrupt, violent halt. Edwin's shoulder was millimeters from serious injury.

He sighed. "Good girl."

Now that the threat was gone. Edwin realized that the strain on the shirt had torn off all the buttons. With the pressure released, Edwin escaped from the tattered remains of his shirt. Still, in tears, Brianna ran to him and hugged him, burying her face in his chest. He embraced her with both arms.

"I'm sorry, grandpa. I'm so sorry."

He patted her back and stroked her hair. "It's okay, Brianna. It's okay."

Chapter Six

Late afternoon on the following day, Brianna was in the shower, shampooing her hair and achieving a maximum of suds. The water sputtered, as usual, its intermittent spurts almost feeling routine until the water stopped entirely. With shampoo on her eyelids, she didn't dare open them.

"Um. Hello? Grandpa? The water cut out again." Receiving no response, she sighed heavily. "Perfect. Come experience the finest in country living. Early sunrises, real farm to fork food, and all the other trappings of the finest lifestyle Backwoods living can provide. Just make sure you take your baths in the creek. If you can find one with water, that is."

Eyes still closed, she fumbled with the water knobs to no avail. No matter which way she turned them, nothing happened. Finally, she turned them off and reached for a towel at the opposite end of the shower. Wiping off her face, she wrapped a towel around herself and was about to step out when she heard Edwin from somewhere outside the house.

"*Damn it!*"

His voice startled her, causing her to misstep. She slipped on the wet tile and crashed to the floor.

"Ow, ow, ow," she cried as she got to her feet and began to dry off her body. "I've got to find some water somewhere. I can't just dry my hair with all this soap in it.

Wrapping a fluffy blue towel around her head, she finished drying off and pulled on a pair of jeans, her short terrycloth robe, and slipped into her running shoes. "If I don't find somewhere to rinse out my hair, I won't be going to that dance Grandpa wants to attend." Leaving the bathroom with a second towel draped over her arm, she left the house and started walking toward the barn, thinking that maybe she could get some water through the hose out there. Approaching the faucet, she turned it on. It sputtered as usual, but the water that came out was brown and brackish.

"Eww! I can't rinse my hair with that."

Desperate, she looked around, seeking water. Then she eyed the horses and the water in their trough. One of the horses snorted at her. She snorted back. "I'm sorry, guys, but I really need this. I promise I won't use any more than I need. Now, where does Grandpa keep that bucket." She searched the barn until she found it. Returning to the trough, she pulled the towel from her head, draping both towels over the top of a stall door. Then picking up the bucket, she filled it with water and bent over in the opposite direction.

Brianna hesitated. She knew this water was going to be cold, but there was nothing else she could do. Raising the bucket, she began pouring it over her head, trying to avoid splashing it on her clothing, but to no avail.

"Oh!"

"Hear, let me help, or there'll be no water left for the horses," Edwin said.

She glanced at him while he refilled the bucket. "Thanks."

When he returned, he slowly poured the water while she used her hands to make sure that the remaining soap was rinsed out. Then wringing it out, she reached for the clean towel and wrapped it around her head.

"Best get a move on," Edwin said. "We don't want to be late."

Edwin's pickup pulled up to the town square and parked among a variety of old and new trucks and cars belonging to the Medford citizens and outlying farmers. The whole area was decorated with festive white lights, and music filled the air. Brianna was mildly amused. This wasn't like anything she had ever experienced and certainly like no other music she had ever heard.

A twangy band, comprised of fiddles, guitars, a couple washboards, a bass, a ukulele, and every sort of makeshift percussion instrument she could think of, jammed with gusto and phenomenal synchrony. In contrast, couples filled the dance floor and danced to the lively beat.

Seeing the expression on her face, Edwin said, "It's a square dance."

" You got that right. A square dance, you're joking, right? Where are we, in Mayberry?" The only reason she knew about Mayberry was because of her mother. Whenever her mother had made fun of her parents, she often would compare them to the characters in an old TV program.

"I'm sure Darryl will enjoy seein' ya."

Brianna frowned, the last thing she wanted was for someone to try and make her dance, she began scanning for him. As she did, a bouncy, 55-year-old, stocky woman named May suddenly grabbed Edwin by the hand. She dragged him into the throng of celebrating townsfolk.

"Edwin! Get in here, you spring chicken!" She exclaimed happily.

"Oh snap," Brianna muttered under her breath. Alone, she eventually spotted Darryl. Trying desperately to disappear into the scenery, while still watching out for

Darryl, she began to notice the men...no, everyone, stealing glances at her. It made her feel like she was on display. So, she pulled out her cell and started texting.

"Well now, you must be the new girl in town," Jed said, startling her.

Oh, please God no, Brianna thought, trying her best to ignore him, but Jed wasn't one to give up quite that easily.

"Edwin's granddaughter, right?"

"Bingo."

"You're a lucky lady. Your grandfather's a good man, solid."

Realizing there was no hope for it, she looked up.

"Name's Jed. Jed Smith."

"Hi, Jed Smith."

"Hi, back. You gotta name?"

"Yep. Brianna."

"Well, pleased to meetcha, Brianna."

"Back at cha, Jed."

They shared a sly grin recognizing kindred spirits.

"Where ya from?"

"L.A."

He scrutinized her slouching curves. "You're bored out of your mind here, ain't cha?"

"Yeah, I am, kinda." She put her phone away. "Why, you know a good party around here?"

"Hm." His visage darkened, but then he smiled. "Nice to meet you, Brianna. I'll be seein' ya."

"See ya 'round."

Out on the dance floor, Edwin's dance with May concluded, and he stepped off the floor, quite winded and holding his chest, but smiling broadly. "Woo, I'm done, May. Thank you much."

"No, sir! Edwin, there's a lot more music…but…"

Her words trailed off as he walked away to explore the crowd, looking for Brianna. He finally found her, but as he moved toward her, Darryl appeared out of nowhere and offered her his hand.

"Evenin', ma'am."

Edwin frowned but left them alone.

"Seriously. Don't ever call me ma'am again."

"Yes, ma'am."

She cocked an eyebrow, incredulous, but before she could say more, he took her hand and dragged her toward the dance floor.

"No, ah, no Darryl, seriously, I don't know how to…."

But it was too late. The next dance had begun.

***

Edwin felt out of place as he stood near the beer kegs with a circle of friends, a couple other farmers, Sheriff Woodbridge, and a trucker. As the men enjoyed their beer and some good conversation, the trucker noticed Jed talking and leaning in quite close to a winsome lass. Their body language suggested that she was enjoying it as much as he.

Edwin also noticed Jed's close-talking.

"No one's safe, now that ol' Cassie up an' disappeared," the trucker commented.

"Lock yer daughters up at night, gentlemen. Wolf's on the prowl," the sheriff said dryly.

The men laughed, but Edwin didn't. He eyed Jed again thinking, *You'd best not be getting' any ideas about my granddaughter, or I'll run ya out of town with my shotgun.* Had he realized that the man had already put the moves on Brianna, he would have been livid.

"An' how am I ever supposed to get my fair shot? Ol' Jed ain't even in the game!" More laughter.

"Ain't supposed to be," Edwin muttered.

***

Brianna was twirled round and round in Darryl's capable arms, half giddy, half mortified. The dance floor was full, but various partners danced effortlessly about one another, a caller directing the action.

As soon as she could, Brianna escaped Darryl and ran off the dance floor. He followed her away from the crowd and out into the starry field. When he caught up to her, he found her crying.

"You okay?"

She turned away from him and sank to the ground, sobbing in the grass.

"I hate this place, and no, I'm not okay!"

"Hate's a pretty strong word."

"Well, look at you! I mean...."

Confused, Darryl looked at himself.

Brianna spoke through her sobs. "With your boots, an' your hanky, and…and that ridiculous hat."

Darryl sat next to her, even more confused. "Um…."

"And horses…horses! I mean, all I ever do is feed chickens and pigs, and garden, and…." She paused to take a deep, shuddering breath. "It's all so revoltingly charming." She broke down again.

He put an arm around her, and she let him.

"And the stars, there are so many of them."

Darryl pointed up. "See them three? That's Orion's Belt."

More quaint charm. She sobbed harder.

"Yeah, Orion was 'The Hunter.' They say you can see this constellation from anywhere in the world."

She tried to dry her eyes, but without a tissue, it was next to impossible, so Darryl handed her his handkerchief.

"Course, that's only what I heard."

"Huh."

"Yeah," he agreed.

She snuggled into him. "Yeah."

He looked down at the top of her head. "What?" He asked softly.

"Oh, nothing."

"Yeah?"

"Yeah," she said with finality.

Darryl smiled. "Yeah.

She pulled her cell phone out of her pocket and turned it off.

Chapter Seven

Still grumbling internally, Edwin noticed an elderly woman, 75-year-old Miss Agnes Flint, across the gathering. He received the beer he had asked for and headed over to her.

Seeing him, Agnes gave him a huge smile, but he did not smile back.

"Edwin! I was wonderin' if we'd be seein' you."

"I'll bet you were, Miss Agnes."

She seemed oblivious to the sarcasm in his voice. "Well now, how is that granddaughter I keep hearing about? I'll bet she just loves living on the farm."

"No, no, she doesn't."

"Really?" His response left her puzzled. "I can't imagine why not. Most young girls would be thrilled to be around horses all the time."

"No, I'm afraid it's a bit too dry for her. She's pretty much hatin' it. Lotta work to be done, what with no water an' all."

"But you still have Darryl. Surely there couldn't be that much work for her to do."

"Yeah, I still have Darryl." He paused a moment. "Thing is, we've got a sight more than twice the work to be done now, though, Agnes."

In the shadows, an obscured man silently eavesdropped.

"Oh? Now, why would that be?" Agnes asked, genuinely clueless.

Edwin's temper flared. "Agnes. My water. The girl can't even take a proper shower without running out of water to wash the soap out of her hair."

His words left her speechless, wondering what on earth he was talking about.

When she still said nothing, he continued.

"It's been shut off, Agnes. Been bone-dry fer weeks now."

"I don't understand."

Edwin grabbed her by the arm. "Why'd you do it, Agnes?"

"Edwin, I don't know what to say. I don't know a thing about any water problems. Why would I?"

"Agnes!"

"I use your hay! Why would I want your water cut off?" She insisted. "That's like cutting off my nose to spite my face."

Edwin felt like he was about to burst. "You didn't cut it off, Agnes. You sold your rights to Satan!"

Agnes froze, horrified by Edwin's outburst. Then with her lips tightly pursed, she said, "I did no such thing, Edwin Bartlett. You should be ashamed of yourself for suggestin' it." She slapped his hand off her arm and stomped off.

Edwin was ashamed of himself, especially when he looked up and saw that people were staring. The Obscured Man, who had been watching from the shadows, slipped away as quietly as he had come.

Edwin moved away from the crowd to a fountain overflowing with water. He looked at it heartsick and slumped next to it. *Ain't right. Just ain't right,* he thought.

***

In the field under the stars, Brianna was lying on her back, hands clasped behind her head, contemplating. Darryl sat beside her.

"Is my grandpa gonna be okay?"

"Don't rightly know."

"Really? Because it looks to me that he's like a minute away from bankruptcy."

"Bankruptcy won't break 'im," Darryl assured her.

"Yeah, but that farm is his whole universe. It's all he has left."

"Nah, there's more to life than money and land, and he knows it."

She looked over and cocked an eyebrow at him. "You know that, and I know that, but I'm not sure grandpa does."

"He knows it, too."

"I thought you knew him really well."

"Look at them stars again."

"Uh, bad timing, Darryl. This is serious."

"Shut up an' listen minute. How come they're so much brighter out here?"

"Because we're totally out in the middle of Thisplacesucksville, in the good ol' U.S. of A."

"Because it's dark out here. An' the darker it gets, the brighter them lights shine. Can't see any of 'em in broad daylight. Things are right in the daytime." He paused. "At night, though, when it's darkest, that's when you can really shine."

"Cheesy."

"If you got any light in you…well, your granddaddy's full of light. You just ain't had the opportunity to see it shine yet."

"So, what you're saying is that things aren't dark enough for him yet?"

"I s'pect the darkness is only just beginning to fall," he warned.

Spooked, she snuggled into him.

Later that night, Edwin finally fell asleep, staring at a picture of his late wife on the bed stand. Although it was an hour later, it seemed like he had just closed his eyelids when a brick smashed through his bedroom window, taking out the picture, and startling him awake. The sound of footsteps receded into the distance outside.

Edwin scrambled out of bed and dashed to the window, but he saw no sign of the intruder. He examined the mess in his room and found the brick. It had a note tied to it that read: *Stop asking questions. Or else.*

After spending the morning on chores and boarding up the bedroom window, Edwin drove his pickup. Which was loaded with bales of hay, into the driveway of the Flint Ranch, he passed Agnes Flint fetching her mail. He tossed her a little wave. She nodded, neighborly but stern.

The pickup drove around the house to the side yard, where Edwin got out and unloaded a few bales of hay. Keeping her supplied regularly was part of an ongoing agreement he had with Agnes. As he finished with the last bale, he looked around. A peeling, rickety, half-decomposed mobile home was parked at the rear of the backyard. Filthy sheets hung in every dark window. Assorted junk was littered about, and near one end of the trailer, beer cans were piled up nearly to the top of the roof. The place was an eyesore. He couldn't understand why Agnes would allow her property to get in this condition. He mulled it over. *Is she getting senile?* He wondered.

Edwin was about to head back to his truck when something about the scene hit him like the brick. Doing a triple-take, he looked back at the scene, focusing on two things. One was a brand new 2020 Ram pickup truck. The other was an old pile of bricks off to the side. Opening the door of his vehicle, he looked again at the block he had set on his front seat. Then he walked over to the pile and examined the ones there. They were a perfect match.

Boiling now, Edwin grabbed the brick from his vehicle, marched to the new truck, and was about to smash it through the windshield, but something held him back. Subduing his rage. He lowered his arm and returned to his truck, placing the brick back on the front seat. The sheriff wanted proof, right? Aside from getting his damaged window replaced, he didn't know how much good it would do him, but he had to try. The brick was proof of a lot more than just a broken window. Maybe Agnes wasn't becoming senile after all.

He looked again at the shiny new truck. Then smiled as he walked toward Agnes' house. A man's face peered at him through a dark, clouded window of the mobile home, watching Edwin go.

Knock. Knock.

Agnes, who had gone back inside after retrieving her mail, was sitting at the table looking through it. She looked up. "Now, I wonder who that is," she said aloud as she stood up and moved to the door, curious.

She had forgotten about Edwin. Opening the door, she said, "Yes?"

Edwin was on the front steps with a small invoice pad in his hand that he had taken from his shirt pocket, where he had placed it this morning after writing out the top one. "Afternoon, Miss Agnes. Got yer hay delivered."

"Thank you." She looked at him blankly.

"Just need your signature."

Stepping out onto the porch, she examined the slip, and then looked at him bewildered.

"It's the invoice."

"Invoice?" She thought for a moment before realization dawned on her. "This wouldn't have anything to do with your outburst last night, would it?"

"No, ma'am. Uh...'bout that. I just...I'm real sorry. I've been under incredible pressure, what with my water bein' cut off and all. And you know, my temper."

"Yes, I know your temper."

"Not that it makes it right."

"But Edwin. We don't do invoices," she protested nervously.

"No ma'am, normally we don't, but it's just the proper paperwork. Way things are; lately, I'm takin' every precaution."

"Well. Can't argue with due diligence," she said, taking his pen and signing the invoice.

He looked at her distinctive signature and gave her the carbon copy. Then scrutinizing every little twitch of her face, he said, "So, you didn't sell off your water rights?"

"No, I most certainly did not!" She said earnestly.

It was clear to Edwin that she was clueless, innocent of the dastardly act that had deprived him of water. He returned to his truck, saying, "Thank you much."

Agnes may have been elderly, but she wasn't ditsy. Something about all this raised her suspicions. "What are you up to?"

But Edwin ignored her as he pulled his rifle from its rack and checked the action. Satisfied, he cocked it and staring daggers, he aimed the gun at the mobile home where the obscure man peered back at him. As soon as he saw the muzzle of the rifle staring at him, the startled man drew back and closed the curtain.

"*Edwin!*"

Ignoring her, Edwin smiled to himself, returned the rifle to its place, and drove away. He had made his point.

***

It was a gorgeous evening. Brianna and Darryl rode horseback along the perimeter of the ranch. She was on her mother's horse, Buttercup. Darryl had been teaching her how to ride. To both of their amazement, she seemed to be natural at it.

"See, you're gettin' the hang of it. Listen, somethin' I been meanin' to say."

Brianna's smiled faded as a 2010 Corvette roared up the driveway to the house. Feeling somewhere between horrified and thrilled, she urged her horse into a gallop toward the house.

"Hey!" Darryl called out as he took off after her. "Careful!"

Having arrived at the house, Brad stepped out of his hot rod, powerfully exuding Beverly Hills money in his rich shades, designer shoes, and chic threads. *Loser* by Beck pounded out of his stereo.

Brianna slowed Buttercup to a trot as she approached him, flush with mixed excitement and embarrassment. She dismounted with impressive agility. Until her foot caught in the stirrup, sending her face-first into the dirt.

"Wow!" Brad exclaimed, half-laughing, but he didn't move to help her up.

"I know my dismount needs work. Shut up."

She went to hug him, but he held her at arm's length, eyeing her freaky ranch duds.

"You're here to save me?"

"What...are you wearing?"

"I know, but hey, it's a ranch. Now shut up and come 'ere."

She wilted, and then knocked his arms out of the way and squeezed him tight. As he hugged her back, Darryl rode up and dismounted. Brianna stepped out of Brad's embrace, clearly embarrassed, not by her actions but by the intrusion.

Darryl eyed Brad with suspicion. "Howdy. Darryl Floyd."

Brad did his best to stifle a laugh. "Howdy. Darryl Floyd, huh. Wow!"

Forgetting about the wonderful time they had spent together and how nice he made her feel, Brianna was mortified by Darryl. All she could think of was that here was Brad. Brad, who had taken the trouble to find out where she lived and come all the way out here to see her. Her actions went back to the way they had been while her mother was alive, and she was struggling to make a new, rich life for herself. She played it as cool as she could, pretending that she barely knew him.

Darryl got the picture and rolled up his sleeves. He wasn't about to back off that easily.

Oh ho! Brad thought. *Does this local yokel really think he has a chance against me?* Popping the trunk of his car, he called Brianna over.

"Hey, baby." He reached into the trunk. "Listen. I'm sorry about...you know. I was such a jerk. So, I thought I'd make it up to you." He pulled out a long, blue, velvet-covered box and handed it to her.

Brianna's eyes lit up as she gingerly opened the box to find a diamond-studded choker inside. She squealed.

Darryl fumed.

"OMG, Brad! You did not! I don't believe this. This is for me?"

"You deserve it, baby. Let me help you put it on."

He did, and Brianna's hand flew to her neck. She couldn't believe how great it felt against her skin.

"Why don't you go look in a mirror? It's awesome on you," Brad suggested.

"Good idea!"

She turned and dashed into the house. Darryl and Brad eyed each other like a couple of elk in rut, waiting to battle it out.

"You the quarterback?" Darryl finally asked.

Brad nodded.

"You buy your girls a lot? It seems like a fancy dude like you should be able to win over a girl without buying her."

Brad's expression turned cold. "Yeah, well, whatever it takes. Right, cowboy?"

Darryl took off his hat and spat on the ground, just as Edwin's pickup rumbled down the drive and pulled up next to the Corvette.

As he eyed the situation, he thought, *If those two roosters don't look ready for a cockfight over a hen, I don't know what does.*

"You're a lucky son of a gun, but I don't know if I would say the same for Brianna," Darryl told the quarterback.

Brad laughed at that, thinking that Darryl was just jealous of him.

Edwin left his truck, frowning at the noise blaring from Brad's speakers.

He looked at Darryl and nodded. Turning to Brad, he said, "howdy."

Brad nearly guffawed. "Howdy!"

Edwin waited for Brad to introduce himself. When that didn't happen, he turned to Darryl. "This a friend of yours?"

Darryl, who was still ready to fight, had an expression of disgust on his face. "Most emphatically no, sir. This here's the quarterback." The word *quarterback* left a bad taste in his mouth.

Turning back to Brad, Edwin extended his hand. "Edwin Bartlett."

"Brad. Brad Wilson." The boy's handshake was reluctant and wimpy.

"Well, what can I help you with, Brad? I reckon you're here to visit Brianna."

"Yeah, just came to...."

His words were interrupted when Brianna appeared at the top of the front steps. Edwin and Darryl were both taken aback when they saw the transformation. She had changed completely, back into her trendiest, most expensive LA costume, complete with a diamond-studded choker. An echo of her mother.

Edwin felt sick.

"Damn, girl!" Brad exclaimed as he admired her beauty.

"Well, what do you think?" She asked Darryl and Edwin.

Darryl's face darkened.

"Prob'ly, not the best getup for feedin' the horses," Edwin said slowly.

"Come on! Isn't it hot?" She could hardly contain her excitement.

"Smokin'!" Brad assured her.

"Don't take no sparkly dog collar to turn up the heat with you, Brianna," Darryl said.

The meaning of his comment flew right over her head. Brianna moved to Brad's side, giving Darryl a pat on the cheek as she went. "Aw, that's sweet."

"Hey, come here," Brad said as he pulled her from the other men around behind a wide tree.

Edwin steamed and glared at Darryl. He could just make out Brad and Brianna's whispering.

"Let me at 'im," Darryl whispered.

Edwin held Darryl's arm and waited, furious but patient. When he heard the apparent sound of smooching, he cleared his throat loudly. Then Brianna giggled. Shortly afterward, the smooching stopped, and Brad and Brianna came out from behind the tree, grinning from ear to ear.

Scrutinizing Brad, Edwin said, "Didja get what ya came for?"

"Edwin!"

Brianna was appalled, but Brad grinned like a fool.

So that's how it is, huh? Yer city slicker boyfriend shows up, and suddenly I'm Edwin again. "Young lady?"

"Boss?" Darryl asked, just waiting to hear the word to take the quarterback out.

Edwin narrowed his eyes and pinned Brad with a look. "When a man comes up to you, you stick out yer hand for a handshake an' you introduce yourself right off! You wanna take my granddaughter aside an' have a little private conversation? You say excuse me, and then, when you're excused, you don't go 'round behind a tree an' have yer way with her!"

Brad grew indignant. "What?"

"Member what I told you, Brianna? Bout that element? Them ninety-nine percent?"

"Just wait a minute," Brad began.

"I like Brad! I love him!"

"You don't even know what love is! You're just a confused little girl trying to grow up all at once."

"Ha! And Brad is not an 'element' you old stiff!"

"How can you speak to me this way? If I had half a mind to, I'd…"

"You wanna go, pops? Right now?" Brianna asked, appalled.

"No! I want you to go to your room this instant and think about the consequences. Think about your future!"

Deeply hurt, Brianna ran into the house crying.

Brad glared at Edwin, while Darryl's waited anxiously for Edwin to give him the nod and run the quarterback off the property. Edwin, however, just paced, trying to cool down, searching for the right words to say.

"Look, mister," Brad began.

Edwin cut him off with a look.

Then Brianna stormed back out of the house, lugging her two suitcases. She marched straight to the Corvette and threw the bags into the still open trunk.

"What in Sam hill do you think you're doing?" Edwin asked her.

64

Darryl was totally bewildered. "Brianna?"

Brad was about to say something, but Brianna cut him off.

"Shut up and get in."

Not one to look a gift horse in the mouth, Brad obeyed and started the vehicle.

"Don't you touch that girl," Edwin hollered. "She's still a minor!" When that didn't stop them, he pleaded, "Brianna! Brianna! Don't do this!"

Darryl leaped onto the hood of the Corvette, but Brad yanked the wheel to one side and hit the gas, easily maneuvering Darryl off the other side.

"Get off my car, you freaking yokel! Damn it! You better not have scratched it."

"Brianna!" Edwin called out once more.

As the hot rod receded into the distance, Darryl picked himself up and dusted off, shaking his head. He knew where this was going, and it wasn't good.

Edwin stared at the trail of dust left behind, anguished over Brianna - the perfect echo of her mother.

Chapter Eight

Zooming over the open road in Brad's corvette, Brianna rode shotgun, her legs draped over the side mirror. She did not, however, feel as carefree and happy as she thought she would. Instead, she stared off into the distance feeling troubled. What had gotten over her back there? She and her grandfather had just begun to make a connection. Now here she was with Brad. What would happen to her? What was she going to do with her life? Where would she live? She supposed she would finish school and graduate, but then what? Was Brad prepared to support her? These questions left her feeling even more unsettled.

***

At the ranch, Edwin climbed the porch steps feeling much like he had on the day his daughter had gone away. It was a nightmare that seemed to be stuck in a loop, leaving him with a heaviness that you could not bear. He was about to clear the top step when a sharp pain seemed to rip through his heart. He stopped, swayed, and held onto a pillar for support, clutching his heart. Fear shot through his veins. He did not want to die. Not yet.

"No, not now. Brianna is going to need me, whether she knows it or not. I have to be here for her."

Then as if by sheer determination, the pain eased, and he continued into the house.

***

The Corvette sailed through the night until Brad noticed that he was getting low on gas. Seeing a sign foretelling of a truck stop ahead, he took the exit and angled the vehicle to the gas pumps. Hopping out, he popped the lock giving him access to the gas cap. A big trucker at the next pump looked over as he filled his gas tank. Seeing Brianna, he stared at her. She saw him and turned to look at Brad, trying to ignore the pervert. She turned down the music so they could talk.

"Why did you come for me?"

"Whoa! She speaks!" When she did not laugh, he continued. "Are you serious? You're the best."

"The best what?"

He removed his credit card from his wallet and inserted it into the appropriate slot on the pump. "Baby, come on. I knew you couldn't be happy out here."

"Yeah, but we don't even really know each other that well."

"Look, I realize I was an ass for turning on you that day. Just because you lived in a dump, doesn't mean you're not hot as hell. You know?"

"*Wow*. So, you came to me because I'm attractive?"

"Obviously. I felt like we'd really started something that could be great. I mean you and me, and it just sucks that it had to be cut short before we even had a chance to really get it on."

Done with this conversation, he rammed the gasoline nozzle into his tank and started filling the car. His actions were almost violent. He liked complacent girls, not ones who asked a lot of questions.

"Do you love me?"

"What? Really?"

Edwin's words came back to haunt her, and Brianna began to see through him.

"No. I mean, how could I? We've only known each other for a short time."

There was a tense silence.

"What if you got me pregnant?"

Brad scoffed. "Whatever! Not gonna happen, okay?"

"Because...?"

"Hey, look. Where is this coming from, okay? This is such a turn-off."

"Where am I going to live? At your house? Are your parents going to be okay with that? If not, where? Do you even care what happens to me as a person?"

"Of course! But the way you're acting right now, I don't even know anymore!"

"Like what? What am I acting like?"

"Like a friggin' public service announcement! Like my mom!" His voice was filled with anger and frustration. He was beginning to feel like he had made a big mistake.

"So, what if I didn't want to have sex?"

"What?"

"You heard me. I'm a virgin. What if I don't want to have sex?"

"Whatever!"

Brianna laughed. "What is it, like impossible to resist you?"

"Unbelievable. I came all the way out here for this?"

"Let me ask you this one question."

"Whatever."

"Seriously." She waited for him to give her his full attention. "Get me a Mountain Dew, will you?" She smiled.

He hesitated, caught off guard, and then cracked a grin and laughed. He turned to go inside. "Sure."

"Oh wait, something else."

He twisted his head around to look at her.

"You only want me for my body?"

Brad's eyes told her everything she needed to know. He went inside. And the lascivious trucker shot her a wink.

***

At the Bartlett Ranch, Edwin struggled into his pickup. He had decided to go after Brianna. He was about to turn the key in the ignition when Woodbridge pulled up beside him in his cruiser. Edwin heaved a deep sigh but remained seated, staring at him through the driver's side window.

"Miss Agnes spoke with me this mornin'." Receiving no answer, he pulled out his cuffs. "I thought we talked about this." When Edwin remained silent, he continued. "Come on, now, you're a grown man.

"Don't patronize me, Allen."

"You brought it on yourself."

"The rifle?"

"Yup."

"Didn't do nuthin' to her. Didn't hurt him. Just went through the motions."

"You can't go about threatening people, Edwin. I told you. I warned you. An' I can't go back empty-handed this time. The Mayor won't stand for it." Woodbridge could see Edwin's pain. "Listen, the big man will make you this deal. Your choice: Come to jail now, or this Sunday, come on back to church."

His words startled Edwin. This was a small town where everybody knew everybody else, including the mayor. They hadn't socialized much since the death of his wife, but he would like to think that they remained on friendly terms. Apparently, they had.

"Been a long time," the sheriff said. "Do it for Brianna."

He never should have said that. Edwin was having none of it. He offered his wrists.

"Think I'd best go on to jail."

Allen's eyebrows shot straight up in amazement. "You're serious?"

Edwin nodded.

Not liking this one bit, Woodbridge cuffed Edwin's wrists. "Where's Brianna? She'll want to know where you…."

"She left."

Dread filled the sheriff, and he was beginning to get a clue as to what was going on. "Left? What, left like Cassie left?"

"Left like Adele left."

"Ouch. I'm right sorry to hear that." Woodbridge finished cuffing Edwin in silence. Then he paused a moment, staring at the ground. "Well. Reckon we ought to send up a prayer."

"Damn it, Allen!"

"You want her to be safe. Don't cha?"

"Experience tells me that prayer ain't a guarantee of nuthin'!"

"No, but...."

"God ain't given me no reason to be in church! An' I ain't gonna waste my breath neither!"

"Look, she's underage. I can send a deputy after her. Do you know where she's headed."

He was about to say more, but a loud noise in the distance stopped him. As it drew closer, the sound grew more distinct. I was loud music and the roaring of an engine. The men looked toward the road.

Brad's Corvette tore down the driveway toward them, the music and engine thundering louder. Woodbridge put a hand on his firearm. He shot Edwin a concerned look. The Corvette pulled up right beside them. Brianna hopped out. Alone.

Half in tears and noticing Edwin's cuffs, she stood there before him, ashamed of herself until finally, she blurted out the words. "I'm sorry."

Edwin offered his wrists to Woodbridge. "What time Sunday?"

Moments later, after taking the cuffs off him, Woodbridge drove off. Edwin and Brianna stood on the top step of the porch, two stubborn individuals yearning for connection.

"Nice car."

Her arm slipped around his waist, startling him. She smiled at him. Edwin smiled back and placed his arm around her, hugging her. She hugged back.

Chapter Nine

Edwin and Brianna pulled up to the Medford Water Master's office and walked in. Fish appeared to be away from his desk, so Edwin headed straight into the file room and searched the drawers until he found what he was looking for. He flipped through several papers until he found the bill of sale, turning Agnes's water rights over to Charles Magnus.

"Here," he said, handing it to Brianna.

"Hey, you can't be in there!" Fish exclaimed as he walked into his office from the adjoining bathroom.

Edwin fished something out of his pocket. It was Miss Agnes's hay invoice.

He placed it next to the invoice and compared it to the signature on the bill of sale. They didn't match. Edwin nodded, solemnly just as Fish hurried around the counter.

"This here's county property! Can't just be…"

"We'll be outta your hair in no time," Edwin assured him.

"It's not her signature?" Brianna asked.

"Forged by her son, I'll wager."

Then Edwin noticed another bill of sale, Jed's.

"Crimin-ney."

"What?" Brianna exclaimed.

Fish snatched away the papers, pushed them aside, and refiled everything. "Dagnabbit, people ought to mind their own business and keep their hands off what's not theirs."

As he walked away, Edwin looked at his granddaughter. "The date. The date Jed gave up his water rights."

"What about it?

Edwin was silent. His countenance fell. He was by no means a stupid person. Thinking back to an earlier conversation at the Medford General Store, everything suddenly made sense.

"What, grandpa?"

"Oh, Jed." He shook his head sadly.

***

Edwin and Brianna had driven over to the Flint Ranch next and were standing at Miss Agnes's door. She stood with them, looking over a photocopy of the forged bill of sale, together with her signed hay invoice.

"This will explain the confusion, Miss Agnes," Edwin told her.

As Agnes perused the documents, she froze for a moment. Then she looked up at Edwin, a befuddled expression on her face.

"It's a forgery," he told her.

"This doesn't explain why you ain't in jail after threatenin' my boy like that. Now git on off my property!"

She stuffed the papers back into Edwin's shaking hands and motioned for them to leave.

"But your son. He forged your signature," Edwin reiterated.

"I beg your pardon?" A look of indignation crossed her face. "He would never!"

"Well, someone did. Just look at the signatures. It had to be him."

"I raised him better than to try and pull something like that!"

"So now you're tellin' me that you've known all along that you sold your water rights to ol' Magnus?"

"Quite."

"Miss Agnes." His voice pleaded with her. He knew she was lying.

"What kinda trouble you tryin' to stir up anyway?"

"But the signature."

"What am I, a Xerox machine, that I can duplicate my signature with perfect precision every time? An old lady gets arthritis! An' I'll thank you very much for reminding me of my age! Git off my porch! Ain't a lick of good in you, is there, Edwin Bartlett? Now git on! An' don't you dare be accusin' my boy of no forgery, you ol' skunk!

Edwin and Brianna retreated to his pickup and drove away.

"I don't understand, grandpa. Why does she deny it? It's so obvious, a little kid could see it."

"Pride," Edwin replied. "She just doesn't want to admit her boy would do such a thing."

***

Agnes slumped against the back wall of her porch, exhausted. She hated the fact that she had lied to Edwin, but she did not want any trouble. After watching them go, she threw a look toward her son's new truck. Her son, the obscured man, appeared at the screen door behind her.

"Don't you worry 'bout a thing, mamma. Everything will be just fine."

She opened the door and walked inside.

74

"Will it?"

***

That evening, Edwin and Brianna sat at the kitchen table, brows furrowed and glistening with sweat. Edwin took the last sip of bottled water, crushed to find it empty already.

Brianna finally broke the silence. "So, we're like, screwed...?"

"One way a' puttin' it."

"Wow."

"Yup."

"Anything I can do to help?"

"Change the subject."

"Okay. I've wanted to ask you about something." Surprisingly, she took his hand and led him into the living room. Brianna sat Edwin down on the couch, shoved an old tape into the VCR, and started it. She then retrieved a large, beat-up cigar box from the drawer of an end table and parked herself next to him.

Edwin recognized the box and immediately flared up. "Where did you find that?"

Brianna pointed to a cupboard. "Back in there."

Edwin stewed as the video played the 27-year-old footage of his much younger family. It showed himself at age 38, his wife, Helen, 28, and little Adele, who was seven, frolicking about the very lush, green Bartlett Ranch. They looked so happy. Next, the video cut to a birthday party with tractor rides, and afterward to fireworks, sparklers, and ice cream sandwiches on the Fourth of July.

Edwin was pierced by the rush of memories. Things had seemed so perfect back

75

then.

"That's my mom?"

Embarrassed, Edwin remained silent.

"I've never even seen a picture of her as a little girl."

"Everything was so green," Edwin moaned.

Brianna opened the cigar box. It was full of teenage girl's old keepsakes. Glancing down at its contents, Edwin was struck again by memories he had locked away and forgotten.

"Damn it, child!"

Brianna took out a little doll. As soon as he saw it, Edwin choked back emotion, it stirred.

"Was this...?"

He nodded, unable to speak.

"Is this all you have left of her?"

He nodded again.

"Me, too."

She gazed at a pressed flower, the colors totally preserved.

"She made that for me," Edwin said.

"She *made* this?"

He nodded

"I had no idea."

He stared at the video. Tears forming.

The video now showed a teenage Adele, 16, shunning the camera in a bright yellow dress under the oak tree with her high school prom date. She was quite animated - a born actress as she smirked away any sentiment.

Edwin dried his eyes, distracting himself with a framed photo on the side table. It was a picture of himself and a few friends, with Jed and his wife, and a blonde bombshell.

Brianna paused the video to look at the picture, amazed. She had never seen her mother look so beautiful. Gently she asked, "What happened?"

At a loss, Edwin replied, "She finished high school and became a woman on a mission."

Brianna let it hang.

"She…" Edwin began and stopped. "This place got to be too small for her."

"You should've seen the dumps we lived in. This place is a castle compared to them."

Edwin cringed at the word *dump*. It hurt.

"Was she happy?"

Brianna's frown crushed him. He suspected that things had been difficult at best. Confirming that was too much. He stormed off to another room.

Sensing he needed some alone time, Brianna studied the photo closer. Something caught her eye. Although Jed stood with his wife, Jane, he actually appeared closer and warmer towards the pert bombshell. Brianna's eyes narrowed. Was he…?

***

Edwin and Brianna sat in a pew next to Sheriff Woodbridge at the Calvary Church of Medford. As a pastor read from the pulpit, Edwin wiped the sweat from his brow and scanned the congregation.

"For now, we see in a mirror dimly, but then face-to-face; now I know in part, but then I shall know fully just as I also have been fully known," the pastor droned on.

Tuning out the sermon, Edwin spotted Jane Smith, Jed's wife. She sat alone.

"But now abide faith, hope, love, these three; but the greatest of these is love," the pastor continued.

Later in the Fellowship Hall, Congregants entered from the sanctuary, shaking hands with the pastor as they went. Folks sipped coffee and munched on cookies, socializing, while children chased each other through the crowd.

The sheriff and Brianna chatted while Edwin sought out Jane.

"Jane."

"Edwin!" She hugged him. "Well, what do you know? It's so good to see you here!"

"Been a long time."

Jane paused, showing genuine concern. "How are you doing?"

"Rather not talk about me. What about Jed? How's he doing?"

"Well, you know, Jed. He's never felt very much at home in a church."

"Hm. Everybody's gotta find their own way, I suppose."

"The Lord will bring him around, I know it. Just a matter of time and prayer."

Edwin cracked a weak smile at her faith. He looked down at the floor and then up at Jane. This was difficult. "He never comes?"

"Like you said. Everybody's gotta find their own way."

"Sure enough."

Chapter Ten

Deeply troubled, Edwin drove toward the Smith Ranch, coughing in the hot dust. The truck wasn't sounding too good, either. As he navigated the long driveway, he saw that Jed's water was overflowing, and he was in the yard, creating additional irrigation. Hearing the sound of crunching gravel, he looked up to see the truck coming toward him.

Edwin pulled up beside Jed and struggled out of his vehicle, wiping the profuse sweat from his brow and moving slowly. Jed continued working.

"Jed."

No answer, although he did hesitate.

"I went to church this morning."

Jed looked up. They surveyed each other, two old friends now estranged. Why?

"Talked to Jane."

Still silent, Jed went back to work.

"Somethin' occurred to me last night. That girl - Cassandra - up an' disappeared right about a week 'fore my water was turned off."

Jed kept his eyes firmly fixed on his work.

"One week before you sold your water rights to ol' Magnus."

No reaction, no response. No eye contact. Jed walked away. Edwin followed, determined to have his say.

"Right after Magnus bought up Miss Agnes's rights, this Cassandra showed up from God knows where. She's here for a coupl'a months, and doggone it if she didn't vanish off the face of the earth one week before you sold your water rights." He let his words sink in. "Jed."

Jed finally turned and faced him. "Look, Ed. I'm sorry about your land, real sorry."

"Everybody's sorry!" Edwin shouted. "Everybody's sorry about my land, Jed, but your pity ain't worth a damn to me right now! How 'bout tellin' me some truth?"

Jed turned his back, but Edwin was determined to get at the truth. He grabbed him and spun him around so that they were standing face-to-face.

"Look at me! You had an affair with Cassie, didn't you?"

Jed's eyes confirmed Edwin's suspicions. It was true, and the fact that his friend somehow found out, left him feeling mortified.

"You're being blackmailed, aren't you? That serpent Charles Magnus reeled in some tart from the city, paid her to seduce you, an' now he's blackmailed you for your water rights!"

Jed refused to confirm, but he wasn't saying no, either. His eyes grew moist.

"She a relative of his? Was she?" When he wouldn't reply, Edwin continued. "Jane doesn't know, does she?"

Fearful, Jed's eyes pleaded with his friend.

"You gotta tell her. You've got to come clean and tell your wife."

"A man can't say nuthin' to you, can he?"

"Jed." Edwin sounded frustrated.

Jed dropped his work and walked away, to the house. "Get your mind out of the gutter, Ed."

***

Digging a ditch was never easy unless you used a backhoe. Edwin didn't have one, so he had to use a shovel. It left him stressed, dehydrated, and sweltering under a blazing hot sun. Brianna worked alongside him. It was grueling labor, but it had to be done. Edwin stopped a moment and wiped his face with a handkerchief. Taking the shovel in hand once more, he continued his labors. Still, as he put his foot on the shovel and dug into the hard ground, his breathing hitched, and he clutched the center of his chest. Pain so fierce it made him gasp radiated from his heart. He collapsed to the ground.

"Grandpa? Grandpa!"

Brianna dropped her shovel and ran over to him, but he was incapable of answering.

"Grandpa! No. No. No."

She pulled out her cell phone and punched in 911, but as she held the phone to her ear, she realized that there was no reception. Of all the things she'd had to handle with her mom – her mother's blackouts, her drunken stupors. Her getting beat up by an alcoholic boyfriend, she had never felt so afraid in her life except for that one day – the day she had come home to find her mother dead at the bottom of the stairs.

"No! Don't do this to me. Please, God. Don't let him die! Please!"

As Edwin lay helpless in the field, Brianna, tears running down her cheeks, raced to the house. With her vision partially blurred, she tripped, hurting her leg and forcing her to hobble the rest of the way.

Entering the house, she said aloud, "Where's that phone?"

There had never been a phone in her mother's apartment. Since everyone she knew owned a cell phone, she was totally unfamiliar with a landline and where one would generally be kept. Being so far out from the city, she thought her grandfather had one, but she had paid little attention to its location. She couldn't even remember her grandfather using it. With rising panic, she looked around the living room. Nothing.

"Bedroom. Maybe it's in the bedroom."

She checked next to his nightstand. No phone.

"Think, Brianna! Where would someone put their landline?"

Then it dawned on her. "The kitchen. Maybe it's in the kitchen."

Running through the house, she entered the kitchen and looked at the countertops. No phone. Brianna began to cry harder. Swinging around in a panic, she finally spotted it on the wall next to the refrigerator. Grabbing the receiver, she jammed her index finger against the buttons.

"911. What is the nature of your emergency?"

"Help! My grandfather collapsed. I think he had a heart attack!"

***

Medics quickly took Edwin's vital signs, placed an oxygen mask on his face, and lifted his body onto a stretcher, which they muscled into an ambulance.

Brianna stood on the sidelines, crying silently and bitterly, fearing a replay of her mother's death. If her grandfather died, what would happen to her? What would happen to his farm? The questions kept coming at her until they overwhelmed her, leaving her numb, her mind a blank. The ambulance drove off, leaving her alone and small in the enormous field.

Tears streaming, she eventually looked about her at the sheer ocean of work to be done. Not knowing what else to do, she picked up her shovel.

Later, with the sun much lower in the sky, Brianna was still digging until the handle on the shovel snapped. Soaked in sweat, she took a moment to rest. She had been digging for hours but had accomplished little. As she rested, she studied the looming estate on the hill.

"This is all your fault," she said aloud. "If you weren't stealing my grandfather's water, he wouldn't have been out here digging in this awful heat. He wouldn't have had a heart attack, and I wouldn't be in danger of losing my home and the only person who cares about me." Infuriated, she marched toward the estate.

Brianna's pace slowed as she neared the foreboding mansion. Looming dark against the sunset, it appeared somewhat frightening. As she approached the porch, she swallowed hard, her courage faltering slightly, she crept up the steps and rang the bell.

A frightened-looking maid named Penny crossed the foyer. She opened the door to find Brianna standing nervous but with practiced composure on the other side.

"Yes?"

"I'd like to see Mister Magnus, please," Brianna said.

"Doctor Magnus? No...no, you don't want to. I...I mean, you really shouldn't. I'm afraid he's not...."

"I have to see him now about my grandfather. He's in the hospital and...."

"But you don't understand. See, Doctor Magnus is...."

"It's okay, Penny," a male voice said from somewhere out of sight. "The Bartlett girl, eh?"

Charles Magnus, immaculately dressed, ancient and rat-faced, with serpentine eyes, appeared, slumped in a wheelchair, and peering around a corner far down the hall. "Welcome her." He rolled out of sight.

Penny stepped aside, reluctantly, allowing their visitor passage. Brianna tiptoed inside, down the long hall, and into the study where Magnus turned a shark-toothed grin on her. He opened an ornate music box sitting on his desk where it danced out a lullaby, delightful but persistent…incessant. It was a tune that once it got stuck in your mind, it could drive you to distraction. She immediately was creeped-out by his presence.

"I have a granddaughter only a few years older than you. I love to play this for her when she visits. Do you like music, Brianna?"

He knows my name? I…I don't know."

"You don't know?"

Brianna felt like a fly caught in a spider's web as she fumbled for the right thing to say. "Well yeah. Of course, I like music."

"Of course," he reiterated, studying her. "Who doesn't?"

Penny entered the room moments later, carrying a serving tray loaded with an assortment of drinks. She glanced oddly, pleadingly, at Brianna until Magnus smiled at her.

"Tea, thank you."

Penny prepared his tea.

"I won't even ask if you're thirsty, child; look at you," Magnus said to Brianna. "We have Earl Grey tea, coffee, orange juice, chocolate milk, cola, ginger ale, and lemonade for starters. And I'm certain Penny can find more in the kitchen if you like."

"Yes, sir, much more," Penny replied.

"N-no, I'm good," Brianna insisted.

"Don't be silly. We're neighbors, and you're obviously parched. You're from the big city, am I correct? How about an espresso? Cappuccino?"

She winced. "Latte?"

"Certainly."

Penny nodded and left to fill the order. Magnus turned that toothy grin on Brianna again. "Now, what shall we talk about?"

Terrified, her next words practically squeaked when they came out. "My grandfather."

"Yes, Edwin. Did you say he's in the hospital? He works too hard for a man his age."

Initially stunned, her courage came rushing back with a flash of anger. "Yeah. Yeah, um...why do you think that is, Doctor Magnus?"

He smiled.

She continued. "I'll bet you have a pretty unique perspective on the whole thing. Gotta pretty good view up here."

"It's not good to be alone in the world, Brianna. I was truly heartbroken when I heard the unfortunate circumstances precipitating your arrival in Medford."

She was stunned again and creeped out. How and why did he know so much about her?

"And even now Edwin, blinded by an absurd zeal for that useless patch of wasteland, has gone and left you all alone. Your only living relative...for the moment." Reading her eyes, he said, "It's true, isn't it, Brianna. Alone again."

Brianna stared at him like a trapped rabbit.

"Careless."

Suddenly, the only thing she could think of was getting away for this horrible person as fast as possible. "I have to go now." She backed out of the room and down the hall toward the front door. "You're like...."

Halfway there, Penny appeared with her latte, but Brianna continued straight past her to the front door. As she let herself out, she finished her sentence.

"...evil."

Chapter Eleven

At the Department of Social Services Dorm, a DSS agent unlocked a large steel door for Edwin. Behind it, another agent stood with Brianna, who rushed into Edwin's arms, nearly toppling him. As they hugged, a tear rolled down his cheek.

"Oh, Grandpa, I was so afraid when you have that heart attack. I thought you were going to leave me, just like mom did. I thought I would never see you again. Are you okay?"

"I'm fine, Brianna. The doctor said it was an angina attack."

"Isn't that almost like a heart attack? You have to be careful and not work so hard. I don't ever want that to happen to you again." She began to cry.

"It's okay, Brianna. I'll be careful."

"Promise? Because if something happens to you, I'll…I'll be all alone, and I don't want that to happen ever again. I need you, Grandpa." She wiped the tears with the back of her hand. "I love you, Grandpa."

"I know, Brianna. And I love you, too."

***

The sun was just setting when the pickup truck pulled up to the farmhouse. Brianna got out of the driver's seat and helped Edwin out the other side. For someone just learning, she had done pretty well, driving slowly and carefully. Fortunately, the ride had been mostly on back roads, where she didn't have to worry about many challenges. She was about to take his arm and lead him into the house, but he motioned for her to go on in without him. Reluctantly, she obeyed.

Looking around, he breathed in the ranch air, taking in the view that had been his world for most of his life. Sweaty and tired, he touched his old tree, the one he had carved a heart into it with his and his wife's initials. That had happened so long ago, a lifetime it seemed. His memories nearly overwhelmed him. Once upon a time, life had been good, filled with love, laughter, and hard work that brought a sense of peace and fulfillment. Would he ever have that again? He didn't think so. All was about to be lost.

With a deep sigh, he walked inside the house and got a bottle of water from the frig. He took a deep swallow and headed for a bookcase in the living room, where he pulled a Bible off the shelf. It had belonged to his wife, and she had read it faithfully every day until she died. Blowing off a coat of dust, he sat and, with trembling fingers, opened it up. Several sections had been marked off with colored ribbons. They had been his wife's favorite passages. He read a few verses, seeking the comfort she had always found in them, but it alluded him.

After reading one verse twice, he looked up and down the hall into a mirror. Edwin could see his granddaughter weeping in her room. Sick with worry for her, he quietly broke down. His heart was too heavy to find any answers in what he was reading.

Although he tried to grieve quietly, Brianna heard him in the other room. She looked out her door, dried her eyes, and crept down the hall toward the living room. Entering the room, she found Edwin drying his eyes. Startled by her sudden appearance, he turned away. The show of emotion on his face pulled at her heartstrings.

"S'okay. I'm okay," he reassured her as he struggled to rise. "There are just a couple things I have to take care of." Leaving the house, he got into the truck and drove off.

Jed sat in a rocking chair on his porch, puffing on a stogie. When Edwin pulled up, he grew tense and grabbed a rifle from beside the door and laid it across his lap. He wasn't sure what to expect out of his former friend at this point, but whatever it was, he wanted to be ready to do what was necessary to stop him. He was determined to protect his secret no matter what the cost.

"Jane? Go see about that laundry for me, would ya?" He called through the door.

"So late?" Appearing at the door, she saw Edwin. "Oh. Certainly."

She disappeared into the house, as Edwin approached and stopped at the bottom of the steps.

"I come...uh. This ain't easy." He paused a moment. "I come to, uh... Well, I come to apologize, Jed. I'm sorry." He indicated the steps. "May I?"

Jed nodded, amazed at the apology. He watched suspiciously as Edwin struggled up the steps and settled into the rocker beside his. Silence ensued for some time before Edwin found the words he wanted to say.

"Well, I got no business comin' down on you like I did."

Still suspicious, Jed gave him a look.

"About that, Cassie business."

"Quiet!" Jed whispered harshly.

Edwin lowered his voice. "Look, I know, all right? I know, Jed. You were set up. Ain't no way you would have given up your rights. Not for no one. Still, you did what you did. But that doesn't give me a license to come down on you like I done. As though I was some bright, shining example." He stopped and took a shaky breath.

Jed was highly agitated and barely moved this whole time.

"This ain't easy," Edwin added.

"You've already apologized. What more do you want with me?"

"Nothin', Jed. You have been patient enough. I know I've been testy. I know it wasn't..." He struggled for the right words. "I just want you to know I don't hold it against you."

"Like hell."

"No, Jed. I...."

Jed's curiosity was aroused. Edwin leaned closer, and so did Jed.

"I had an affair once, too," Edwin whispered agonizingly.

"On Helen?"

Edwin nodded, a tear forming. He fought it back. "Been hidin' it most of my life. Well, I'm sick of the dark secret. I'm sick of it eatin' at me. So, there it is."

Jed said nothing. Tensing again, he puffed on his stogie. "If you think that's gonna change anything. It don't."

"This Cassie thing...Don't cha see he's got you by the throat?" Struggling to his feet, Edwin hobbled to the steps. "Listen, I only wanted you to know that I don't hold myself up like some kinda saint." He stopped to take another breath. "And you ain't alone."

Jed's eyes bored into Edwin's. "You know I've been considerin' a restraining order?"

***

Edwin drove off heartbroken. He had hoped that Jed would come clean. He hadn't. Had Jed ever truly been a real friend? He wondered because it seemed that he did

not care about anyone but himself. With his and Brianna's welfare at stake, he was

willing to try anything to stop this nightmare from happening. As he headed for his next

destination, the pickup sputtered severely. *The truck's just like me,* he thought. *It's on its*

last legs.

Twenty minutes later, he arrived at Miss Agnes's farm. Easing from his truck, he

crossed the short distance to the porch and stood on the stoop feeling diminished. He

knocked on the door. She answered it in a nightgown and robe. Seeing who it was, she

silently glowered at him.

"Uh. About disturbin' you so late like this Miss Agnes, I uh, I'm sorry."

Her eyes went wide with surprise. "What? I…I'm sorry, can you repeat that? Must

be my age."

"Miss Agnes, I'm sorry."

"Huh!"

"I hadn't considered your position. Well, I'm sure you remember that I had a child

of my own once, too. Adele. She was…she died." He paused, carefully framing his words

so that, hopefully, they would hit the mark. "I know you're afraid. I was, too. You wanna

raise 'em right, but sometimes you just can't …You wanna protect 'em." He began to

weep. "But there's only so much you can do."

Agnes softened. She was typically a kindhearted soul, and seeing him so

distraught touched her heart.

Edwin struggled on through the tears. "We never talked." He shook his head. "I

never took the time to just talk to her."

Agnes put her hand over her mouth but kept her distance.

Edwin understood and backed away. "Anyway. I just wanted to say that I'm sorry. Good night."

She nodded sternly, but she was baffled.

**

The next morning, Edwin left his house with the last dregs of bottled water and surveyed his land, walking through the stables, past the waterline, and by the dry pond.

The well diggers were hard at work when he strolled past, giving them a nod. They watched and pitied him, returning to their work without a word.

Returning to the porch, Edwin touched the old railing and looked out over the ranch once more.

Brianna watched from a window but then disappeared. Reappearing when she walked through the front door and onto the porch. "You okay?"

Edwin checked his watch. "I don't believe I have any other choice. I guess I'd better get this over with."

Chapter Twelve

Edwin climbed the hill to the looming mansion. In his current state of mind, it seemed longer, steeper. When he reached the porch, he climbed the steps, rang the bell, and waited. After a minute, Penny opened the door, and without a word, bid him enter, leading him down a long hallway toward the back of the house. Edwin trudged into the absurdly large, bright room. Its windows afforded an equally absurd view of Edwin's land.

Stopping in the center of the room, Penny turned to him and said, "Dr. Magnus will be with you in just a moment."

As soon as she left, Edwin approached a wide bank of windows and gazed across the lush green lawn at his ranch. Once upon a time, it had been lush and green, too.

"I'm sorry this decision has been such a difficult one for you, Edwin."

Edwin turned to find Magnus in his wheelchair in the doorway, his attitude superior and insufferable as he studied the broken man before him.

"I hope it hasn't affected your health." The lies rolled off his tongue like honey.

"Decision? I don't see as to how I had much of any say in the matter."

Magnus's only response was a grinning, smug stare.

It infuriated him. "What decision? You've manipulated situations, manipulated people, twisted and hurt them to get what you want."

"Come now, Edwin. Don't we all?"

"No. Most people around here respect each other. They have a healthy soul. Yours is blacker than sin. A rot festering within you that is eating away at your physical body. Only you are too blind to see it." His words had no effect, so he blurted. "You're blackmailing Jed!"

"Blackmail?" Magnus asked. "Blackmail is such a strong word. Don't you think? A person should go around accusing people of things that aren't true."

"Don't even start trying to lie to me, Magnus!" Edwin said fiercely. "You set him up! Jed! Everyone knows his eyes have a way of wanderin'. So, you had him seduced! That girl Cassie, is she a relative?"

"Truly, you are a spring of mysteries, Edwin, but your paranoia hardly justifies such an accusation."

"Ain't paranoid, I'm backed into a corner! And if you think you ain't gonna get a fight from me, well, then you're just crazy."

Magnus saw the man standing before him as having little more importance than a petulant child. "I want to help, Edwin. Really I do."

"Ha! Blackmail's illegal, case you hadn't heard."

"Indeed. However, I haven't blackmailed anyone."

"Prove it!"

Magnus' smile widened. "Prove that I have."

Edwin turned to the windows, stumped. "How much you give that boy to forge Agnes's signature?" He turned back to face his nemesis. "Why not forge it yourself? One less witness to the deed."

"Tsk, tsk. Forgery is illegal."

"My point exactly!" Edwin shouted, losing his temper.

"Penny?"

Penny appeared at the doorway. "Yes, sir?"

"My cane, please."

"Certainly."

She left the room briefly, handing it to him upon her return. He placed it defensively across his lap. The way he did it spoke volumes. Edwin understood the warning.

"Farley, would you mind stepping forward?"

A 6'8" hulk-in-a-suit entered the room. He had been waiting just outside the door, in case he was needed.

"I'm afraid I'm going to have to ask Farley to frisk you, Edwin. What with your penchant for firearms and all."

Farley loomed over Edwin and frisked him. Utterly humiliated and physically helpless against such a massive man, there wasn't anything Edwin could do but endure it.

"Aw, come on. I'm not...." His words were interrupted by the not so gentle patting down of his person.

Magnus looked at Penny. "Do you have your cell phone on hand?"

She nodded.

"Stay close."

"Yes, sir."

Finished, Farley stood guard beside his employer.

Deflated, Edwin sighed. "I just want what's mine."

"Of course."

"Doublespeak all you want, but you and I both know you been doin' wrong here. I just can't figure out why." He paused before continuing almost under his breath. "I just want what's mine."

"Do we have any tea, Penny?"

"Of course."

She left, and Magnus turned back to Edwin with a smile. "Thirsty?"

Edwin looked at the floor, mustering every ounce of self-restraint he possessed to keep from striking out. He was boiling mad.

An incredible silence followed with only the sound of Penny's work penetrating the stillness from clear across the house and the ominous tick-tock from a clock on a side table. Magnus eyed it.

11:46.

Edwin looked out the window again, his imagination seeing his ranch as green and lush, swarming with strong ranch hands working the fertile land. Little Adele frolicked with their dogs as Helen and Edwin walked along behind, hand-in-hand. He snapped back to the present to see the dry, parched land that lay beyond Magnus' estate. It was nothing more than a precious memory, one he wasn't sure he could hold onto once the land was no longer his.

Penny returned with a tray full of drinks and the contract. Magnus took his tea and offered the tray with the contract to Edwin.

"See anything you like?"

Edwin scowled, ignored the drinks, and rubbed his face, deliberating. What choice did he have? He picked up the pen with trembling fingers and hesitated once more.

"I know you didn't come up here to try to talk me out of this. You knew you were going to sign before you came." He took a sip of tea and smiled like a shark swimming in for the kill. "No shame in that."

Ding dong.

Penny scurried out of the room, heading for the door.

"Ah, my register of deeds is early," Magnus announced.

It wasn't the person he expected, however. Brianna ran into the room.

"Miss. Miss! You can't go in there."

"Grandpa!" She called running up to Edwin.

"What's the meaning of this?" Magnus shouted. "Penny, how did this girl get in here?"

"Brianna?" Edwin was puzzled by his granddaughter's appearance.

Penny did not respond. She was still occupied by several other people also at the door. "Doctor Magnus is in a meeting. You'll have to make it...Hey!"

The new arrivals pushed past her, and seconds later, Jed entered the room, followed by Agnes.

"Just because we wasn't invited, don't mean we shouldn't be here," Jed said.

Brianna looked into her grandfather's eyes. "I talked them into coming."

Now Magnus laughed. "What on earth for? Are *they* going to try to talk me out of this? No one here is in any position to help you, my friend," he said, looking at Edwin. His eyes locked with Jed's. "I'm sure that I don't need to remind you that if anyone speaks out of turn, you will both have a great deal to lose."

He turned his gaze to Agnes. "Of that, you can be certain."

Penny hurried into the room, and everyone grew silent, suddenly feeling foolish.

"Penny, you didn't invite them in, did you?"

She shook her head, no.

"Then it is time to use that phone. Dial the police. They're trespassing."

She stepped out to obey.

Jed took a deep breath to steel himself for what he was about to say. Seeing Edwin with the contract and pen, he said, "Put down that pen, Ed." He turned to Magnus. "You've got no more leverage. He already knows what I have done, or rather, what you done."

"Penny!"

Penny returned, still on the phone. "Yes, officer, as quickly as you can. Thank you." She punched off the phone. "Yes, sir?"

"Dial Jed's wife, Jane Smith."

She looked up the number.

"Won't do you no good. Jane already knows, Charles. I told her."

Magnus did his best to hide his shock. "No matter. I still have your signature."

"Your contracts with Jed and Agnes won't hold up, Magnus. Blackmail and forgery don't fly in this town."

"You should be ashamed of yourself!" Miss Agnes said, putting her hands on her hips and giving him a searing look.

The sheriff's cruiser pulled up outside and parked.

"Just as unacceptable in this town, Miss Agnes, are coercion and trespassing," Magnus informed her.

The bell rang, and Penny left to get it.

11:59

Determined to bluster his way through this, Magnus looked at Edwin. "You have fifty-three seconds."

Sheriff Woodbridge entered the room just as he finished speaking. "He's got his whole life. Your illegal manipulations are well documented, sir. I'm afraid your water rights aren't yours anymore. Never were. Agnes, Jed, you got your rights back."

"Maybe so, but I have a question. Is it not true that accepting a bribe can land a young man up to...what is it? Fifteen years?"

"My boy done landed himself in plenty of trouble, Chuck. This mornin' he held up the General Store," the sheriff proclaimed. "Looks like he will be doing plenty of jail time for armed robbery."

Brianna turned to her grandfather. "I called the Sheriff this morning, too."

Edwin and Brianna hugged. It was finally over, and Magnus was finally going to get what he deserved. Oh, his money and lawyers would probably get him out of most of it. But never again would he be able to threaten the good people of this valley.

***

Edwin, Brianna, Jed, Miss Agnes, and Sheriff Woodbridge descended the hill toward Edwin's ranch, laughing and cheering. The weight that had been taken from them made them feel as though they were flying.

Darryl suddenly appeared out of nowhere, racing up the hill toward the gang, followed by a well digger and his foreman.

"Ed! Edwin!" Darryl shouted triumphantly. "You're not going to believe this!"

"You were right! We just needed to go deeper!" The foreman told him.

Everyone rushed over to the dig-site for the new well and gathered around. The well diggers slapped Edwin on the back, grinning from ear to ear. Afterward, the gang headed over to the pond to find clear, fresh water shooting out the pipe, filling the pond. Brianna slipped off and brought three of the horses down for a drink.

"Like that? Good, huh?" She asked, seeking her grandfather's approval.

He smiled and nodded as Darryl joined them again.

"Howdy," Darryl called out.

"Howdy!" Brianna replied happily.

"How you likin' this weather?"

"I love fall! It's gorgeous." Happy and carefree at last, Brianna looked stunning.

"Beautiful," he replied, but he wasn't looking at the scenery.

She blushed.

***

Days later, Edwin and Brianna walked the ranch in the early evening before sunset. She wore a colorful, cardboard, cone-shaped birthday cap, avoiding the sprinklers spread all over the place, spraying water. The green was returning at a faster rate than anyone expected. All thanks to those precious drops.

"It was a good birthday, the best one ever. Thank you."

"It was," Edwin agreed, contented. It had been a long time since he felt so happy.

"So, while you were in the hospital, I had some time to think."

"I'll bet you did."

"Hey now, I did my chores," she protested.

He smiled.

"And, well…I kinda like some of them."

Edwin's face showed a mock surprise. "My, what is this world coming to?"

"I know. Right?"

"Can't feed chickens in L.A."

"Probably not," she agreed.

"Do they even have chickens in Beverly Hills?"

Brianna laughed. "Only in grocery stores and restaurants."

"Funny, I thought them restaurants only had duck and lobster, some steak, maybe. Oh, and that free-range, escargot-fed steak, too."

Brianna laughed again. "They can have it. I want to stay here."

"Whoa. Here? To live?" At that moment, his love for her swelled even greater.

She nodded.

"I think that'd be fine…just fine."

Brianna hugged him fiercely. "And maybe I could decorate the place a bit?"

"Oh, the lady's touch. I see."

"It'll be good. I promise Grandpa."

"Yes," Edwin replied tenderly. "It will."

www.ingramcontent.com/pod-product-compliance
Lightning Source LLC
Chambersburg PA
CBHW022043170626
46808CB00003B/1347